“I’ll walk with you,” Nate said.

“I’m fine. I just live a few yards behind this house.”

“I know. But it’s a clear night. We might see some stars.”

“An irresistible lure,” Annika said with a smile.

“I think so, too.” He clasped her by the elbow with a strong, warm hand and guided her to the door. He led her outside and stopped when they reached the front gate of the house. “Look up there. Not a cloud in sight. We just might get lucky and see a shooting star if we stand still and keep our eyes on the night sky.” Head raised, his face shone under a bright moon.

He was...indescribable. Handsome, but beautiful, too, inside and in the way he thought of others. A keeper for any smart and lucky woman. Annika edged closer to him, wishing she were that woman.

“There!” he exclaimed, turning to her. “Did you see it? A shooting star, just over the woods.”

She shook her head and looked up just as Nate bent down and kissed her, and the night sky disappeared...

Dear Reader,

Stealing the Sheriff's Heart is the fourth book in my Home to Maple Glen miniseries, set in the fictional village of Maple Glen, near the Appalachian Long Trail in Vermont. I enjoyed creating Maple Glen and populating it with the kinds of complex and complicated characters we meet in real life. In a Harlequin Heartwarming novel, all problems are resolved through honest communication and proclamations of love, but getting to that important step proves challenging for Sheriff Nate Gallagher and Annika Morrison.

An unhappy work experience and a family secret have brought Nate to Maple Glen. He takes the job as interim sheriff mainly to solve the puzzle of his childhood. Falling in love was definitely not part of the plan, especially when that love interest is a woman who threatens to expose a dark side of Nate's past.

Annika Morrison is determined to kick-start her shaky career as a podcaster for a large media corporation, and her discovery of Nate's background could provide the material she needs to succeed. But is she willing to risk losing the man she has come to love in order to achieve that goal?

I hope you like their journey!

Janice Carter

STEALING THE SHERIFF'S HEART

JANICE CARTER

Harlequin
HEARTWARMING

Harlequin® HEARTWARMING™

Recycling programs for this product may not exist in your area.

ISBN-13: 978-1-335-60527-6

Stealing the Sheriff's Heart

For questions and comments about the quality of this book, please contact us at CustomerService@Harlequin.com.

Harlequin Enterprises ULC
22 Adelaide St. West, 41st Floor
Toronto, Ontario M5H 4E3, Canada
www.Harlequin.com

HarperCollins Publishers
Macken House, 39/40 Mayor Street Upper,
Dublin 1, D01 C9W8, Ireland
www.HarperCollins.com

Printed in U.S.A.

1 2 3 4 5 6 7 8 9 10 HDC 29 28 27 26

Janice Carter has been writing Harlequin romances for a long time, through raising a family, teaching and on into retirement. This is her twentieth romance and she has plans for many more—along with plenty of personal family time, too.

Books by Janice Carter

Harlequin Heartwarming

For Love of a Dog
Her Kind of Hero
His Saving Grace
The Christmas Promise
The Officer's Dilemma

Home to Maple Glen

A Small Town Fourth of July
Rescued at Christmas
A Family for Valentine's

Visit the Author Profile page
at Harlequin.com for more titles.

For my lovely family

PROLOGUE

The wedding invitation was propped against the top row of books on the shelf above her desk where she'd placed it almost three weeks ago. Annika stared at it, feeling the tug of guilt that flared and died each time she looked at the crisp white envelope. She snatched it up and, plopping onto her sofa bed, lifted the envelope flap and pulled out the card inside.

Maple Glen. The village was far away from New Hampshire and hardly a tourist destination. She'd searched it online months ago when she'd first learned she had a connection to the place. She studied the thick white card with its childlike sketch of a big old-fashioned house surrounded by trees.

You are invited to...

When she'd received it, she'd had no intention of going, but now the invite, the location and the current circumstances of her life made all the difference. What was a glen anyway? She reached for her cell phone and seconds later had the answer—*a small valley surrounded by mountains.* Mountains. Off the beaten track. Even better.

Annika withdrew the second, smaller card with RSVP info and the email address she'd received when she'd learned she had a half-sister—Devon Fairchild—living in Maple Glen, Vermont. Other than a couple of emails, prompted by the social worker who'd tracked down her half sibling, there'd been minimal communication between them.

The stunning revelation came soon after she and Liz, her best friend and fellow podcaster, were wrapping up their podcast series—*We Reveal It*—for Venture Media. At the time, their contract with the media giant had yet to be renewed and now, never would be, thanks to pressure on the company from influential businesspeople. When Venture Media turned down their pitch for a second series on political corruption in small-town America, Liz had advised her to "take some time in a far-off place where no one knows you, until things cool down."

Well, someone in Maple Glen *did* know her. Kind of. They had yet to meet face-to-face, but their bond was strong. *Family.*

The rejection of the new podcast pitch wasn't

only a blow to her ego, but to her current and dismal financial situation. Now a new opportunity had just surfaced, thanks to an unexpected wedding invitation from the half-sister she had yet to meet. In a place called Maple Glen. There would be a place to stay and perhaps even a story to discover.

CHAPTER ONE

"WELCOME TO MAPLE GLEN!"

Nate smiled at the portly gray-haired man handing him a ledger book that looked as though it had been bound in the 1900s. The man himself—Bernie—in his well-worn, faded jeans held up by red suspenders and partially covered by a grimy apron, could have been transplanted from another era as well. Judging by the state of the apron, perhaps a cook in some nineteenth-century tavern.

"Just fill in the general info," Bernie said.

Nate shook himself back to the present. "Oh, right." He took the ledger book, staring down at the lined and columned page with its various headings—date, name, home address and length of stay—and information scrawled by hands that Nate figured were more used to keypads. He filled in everything but his address, which he deemed unnecessary and noticed others must have felt the same. Besides, he actually no longer had one.

"Sit over there." Bernie pointed to a wing

chair next to a small table that Nate knew his mother would have loved. He peered around as he sat, taking in the furnishings from another era, too.

"You said a week?"

"Maybe less. Hopefully that's all I'll need to find a more permanent place and settle in."

"Settle in? So…you're planning to stay in Maple Glen?"

Nate saw the rise of curiosity in the man's face and was tempted to let him in on the reason for his arrival in the village but resisted. The residents of Maple Glen would learn all about him soon enough, but until then, Nate hoped to enjoy—even profit from—his current anonymity. "Well, I love small towns and have some vacation time so…you know…" His vague shrug only deepened Bernie's frown.

"Hmm, well, I'll leave you to this while I get my bread out of the oven."

"Bread?" Nate's head shot up. His stomach reminded him of the lackluster breakfast he'd had at a roadside diner on his way south from Montpelier.

"I just bake for my breakfast service. Don't like to compete with my friend, Sue Giordano, who runs the Tasty Delights Bakery."

"I think I passed that bakery. There was a line

out to the street." He planned to be in that line as soon as possible.

"Tourist season. Normally Wednesdays are slow for business there."

"Do you get a lot of tourists here? I mean…"

"Too small, you're thinking?" Bernie smiled. "It's because of the proximity to a section of the Appalachian Trail at the end of the road. Kind of a shortcut, so some day-hikers start their walk here." The frown reappeared. "Problem is they leave their vehicles on our main street out there and even on the county road leading up to Route 7. Causes all kinds of problems for the locals when they want to shop and park here in the village. Which reminds me…did you come by car? If so, I own the small lot east of here and you can park there. I'll need the plate number and so on."

"Sure." Nate felt a spark of interest at Bernie's comment about the current issue in the village. Perhaps his new job wouldn't be as dull as he'd expected. He was tempted to ask questions but figured the problems Bernie Watson hinted at would land on his own shoulders soon enough. He had almost a week before that inevitability, and he intended to make full use of the time.

"I provide breakfast," Bernie went on, "and will do lunch, if necessary, but for other meals you're best going into Wallingford. The bakery does pizza and other things like potpies and quiches." After a slight pause, he added, "I'll leave you to it, then. Here's the key. Yours is the only room on the third floor. Top of the stairs to your right. Separate washroom right next to it, if that's okay. I don't have many ensuites."

Nate tucked the small brass key into his shirt pocket. "How old is this house?"

"Built in the mid-1800s, but it's not the oldest home in the Glen. That would be the McAllisters'—the Manor, they used to call it. If you're interested in history and old things, you've come to the right place."

"*Interesting* local stories?"

"Well, there's definitely a lot of stories here, some old and some new. Interesting would depend on who's hearing the story I guess." Bernie shuffled toward the doorway, turning around briefly to add, "Leave that book on the table when you're finished. You can pay the deposit on the room later. Oh, and breakfast is from eight to ten down here, across the hall." He peered at his wristwatch. "Now I need to see to my bread."

"Okay and uh, one more thing," Nate craned round as Bernie headed for the door leading into the hall. "I noticed the balcony or whatever it is on your rooftop. Is it accessible?"

"The widow's watch, we call it in these parts. It's accessible but I can't guarantee the safety of the railing. Why do you ask?"

"Just that I'm an amateur astronomer and I brought my telescope with me. The night sky here must be wonderful, so far from any big city."

"It can be. I'm not sure late October is the best time for stargazing, but what do I know?" He gave a light chuckle. "The entry to the roof is in the ceiling of the landing right outside your room. There's a hatch with a handle and if you give it a tug a small ladder will drop down. It's old and rarely used anymore. No one's been up there in years. We haven't had much snow yet, so I reckon the roof will be accessible enough, but I'll get Finn McAllister to pop around and inspect everything first. Don't go up just yet."

"I won't."

After Bernie left, Nate finished his basic details and set the ledger book on the table. His rise of excitement about the rooftop was slightly dampened by the promise to wait for someone to inspect it. Nate heard only part of the man's name, because his attention had focused on the term Bernie had used for the walk-out. *Widow's watch.* Clearly a relic from the past, and one he'd have to Google. He retrieved his suitcase and telescope case from the entryway and headed upstairs, noting the gleaming oak staircase and banister. The B and B was clearly well tended and loved by its owner.

The staircase ended on the second floor and Nate walked toward the continuation of the stairs at the end of the hall. He counted three bedrooms on each side, and his would be a seventh. The place was the smallest accommodation he'd ever stayed at, a random fact that appealed to him. He'd never been a fan of five-star hotels, not even the boutique kind, a term he found pretentious. What did it mean, exactly? Small but costly, he reckoned. The Shady Nook seemed, thus far, exactly what he was looking for. The bonus was its location right in the middle of Maple Glen, providing him with a bird's eye view of the place, with a little help from his telescope if necessary.

He unlocked the door and gently pushed it open, pausing on the threshold to take in the room. Old-fashioned definitely, but not the stuffy, chintz-covered furnishings normally attached to the term. No lace doilies or antimacassars. Nate gave a sigh of relief at the modern double bed—not a four-poster canopy, thank goodness—and loved the two gabled windows at the eaves, giving plenty of light, not that he'd be spending his daytime hours here. There was a medium-sized desk under one of the gables with a spindly-looking chair, which Nate already knew he wouldn't be using, a small chest of drawers and next to it, a settee which didn't look sturdy enough to hold anything heftier than a cat. He smiled. Basically, it was his kind of room.

An hour later, he was in line at Tasty Delights Bakery. The queue wasn't long, and Nate suspected that soon people might even stand aside to let him go ahead. Not that he'd take advantage of any deference to his station—in fact, he wouldn't even like it—but over the years he'd accustomed himself to the way people behaved around him. Which was another reason to enjoy some anonymity while he could.

There was a young man waiting on customers and a middle-aged woman, arms crossed, was standing next to him behind the counter. Her expression was serious, as if she were not only judging the fellow's abilities but even the people in line. A very tall broad-shouldered man a few customers ahead of Nate reached the counter and was greeted by big smiles from the woman and her clerk.

"Hey, Finn! The usual?" the woman asked.

Nate's ears twitched at the familiar name. He angled his head to peer over the shoulders of the two women ahead of him, noticing for the first time that the man was wearing some kind of uniform.

"You betcha, Sue. Busy today, for a Wednesday," the man commented and briefly turned his head to the line behind him.

Nate watched Sue lower her head toward the man—Finn.

"Tourists arriving for the fall colors and I hear some have even come for Thanksgiving, still a month away," she commented in a low voice. She bent to reach for a pastry in the glass-covered case and, popping it into a paper bag, handed it to Finn. "On the house," she said as he opened his wallet.

Nate was intrigued. Was this a regular occurrence or a one-time thing? Sue immediately provided the answer.

"Seriously. I appreciate the business you and Devon have given me and please tell her the wedding cake will be delivered to the Manor the Saturday morning of Thanksgiving weekend. Also, the rest of her order has been passed on to my catering source in Bennington, and everything's arranged, with servers and so on. Is there anything else I can do for you two?"

Nate heard the man chuckle as he shook his head.

"Other than make time go faster, that's it. Thanks, Sue, and see you again soon."

When Finn turned around to leave, Nate noticed the badge—Wallingford Fire Department—on his jacket. He could have stopped him right then and there to ask about the Shady Nook rooftop but knew a bakery full of customers wasn't the place for that discussion. Plus, he preferred to hang on to as much of his personal life as possible and for as long as possible. Given the size of Maple Glen, he figured as soon as he revealed himself as Otter Valley's interim sheriff, any chance of a private life would quickly vanish.

He spent the next couple of hours settling into his room and then conducting an internet search for the names of the few people he'd encountered so far. Sue Giordano. Finn McAllister. Bernie Watson. Nothing surprising or unexpected with any of them. Lastly, he typed in another name—the one that had spurred him to apply for the sheriff's job. Walter Ingram.

The website for Walter Ingram's Honey House filled in some of the blanks from the letter he'd found in his mother's safe-deposit box after her will had been probated. That letter was in a folder in his backpack, but he knew the details by heart.

> My dearest Nate, I want to apologize for passing on this information after my death but knew I couldn't bear to answer the hundreds of questions you would ask—police work is definitely your forte!—and so have taken the cowardly way out. You know

me…avoiding confrontation whenever possible. When you were little, you asked me about your father and your curiosity was painful for me, because you were too young to understand how adults get themselves into situations that can end badly. But you were my happy ending to a situation I've never regretted—loving a man who could never be mine.

That man was Walter Ingram, and he lives in a village called Maple Glen in Vermont. It's on the map and you should be able to find it. But Walter doesn't know about you—if he had known, he'd have pursued a connection, which would have affected our family life and I didn't want that for you, me or Paul, who was a good stepfather until our divorce.

Please forgive me if this information causes you problems. I simply wanted you to make the decision to contact Walter when you were an adult. You've been the best son a mother could possibly want, and I wish you happiness and true love in your life, wherever you find it.

Love,
Mom

The discovery of the letter happened to coincide with Nate's resignation from Boston Police following his report about a small group of fellow officers accepting bribes from neighborhood businesses. He'd known when he made the decision to pursue the matter that his career could be jeopardized and, after a subsequent meeting with police administration, opted to resign rather than be transferred to another precinct.

When he saw the online posting of sheriff in an area of Bennington County that included Maple Glen, he immediately applied. There was nothing Nate enjoyed better than a bit of detective work, and here was an opportunity to continue policing, and especially, to learn the truth about his family history.

CHAPTER TWO

ANNIKA PURPOSELY DELAYED going down to breakfast her first morning at the Shady Nook B and B, fearing that the guest whose telescope she'd used last night would be in the small dining area and she'd be forced to apologize for her behavior or, worse, explain why she'd been spying on the street and houses below. Not that she'd seen much anyway. The settings weren't adjusted for such close viewing and only revealed blurred images. It had been stress about meeting the half-sister she'd only recently learned about—Devon Fairchild—that had led to her impulsive use of the telescope. Being discovered by the telescope's owner had been especially embarrassing, and she'd rushed away rather than have to offer an explanation.

Fortunately, the dining room was empty, and she sat at the only table that was still set for breakfast. She checked the time on her cell phone, noting there were exactly ten minutes remaining before breakfast service ended. Seconds later the owner—Bernie, she recalled—appeared in the doorway between the kitchen and dining room.

"I only have a couple of guests at the moment," he said, "so I didn't make a lot of breakfast. But I can fry up some eggs, plus there's toast and Marion McAllister's homemade strawberry jam, if you like."

McAllister, as in Finn, as in Devon's fiancé? The size of Maple Glen clearly involved many connections and interconnections, and Annika, a born and bred big-city person, wasn't sure how she'd like that.

"Coffee?" she replied, hearing his slightly impatient sigh.

"There's always coffee." His smile made up for the sigh. "That's it?"

"Maybe some toast and jam. I'm not a breakfast person really."

He nodded and was about to leave when he turned around to say, "Did you note how long you might be staying when you checked in last night?"

"I think I wrote a couple of days in your book but I'm not sure just yet." She left an explanation hanging, knowing she had yet to meet up with Devon. Her sister's last email had extended an invitation to stay at the Manor with her and Finn, but Annika had stalled, preferring to get to know her a bit first. Plus, she'd want more privacy and independence, especially if her new podcast idea for Venture Media panned out. On the other hand, taping from the Shady Nook wouldn't be ideal, although its quaintness had already inspired her to include it—maybe even Bernie himself—in an early episode.

She scrolled through her text messages while Bernie was making her toast and was relieved to see the most recent from her friend and podcast collaborator, Liz, saying that she'd managed to find a suitable sublet for Annika's share of the house they'd been renting in Concord, New Hampshire. The best news was that Liz had found another job writing for an online community newspaper there, which eased Annika's guilt about losing the contract with Venture Media.

After she sent thumbs-up and heart emojis, she searched for more information about the village of Maple Glen, the larger town of Wallingford, and Bennington County itself. The website for Maple Glen simply showed a photograph of a one-story building labeled Community Center with a Donate Now sidebar. A column titled Upcoming Events listed a Halloween Haunted House for children ages seven to ten and a Halloween Dance for teens. A small box beneath the column asked for volunteers to accompany groups of children (eleven years and younger) trick-or-treating in the Glen. Annika gathered there was a lack of interest in maintaining the village site because the brief information about Halloween was the only current posting.

A text notification from Devon suddenly popped up and Annika read the one-line message—Come for dinner tonight!—as Bernie returned with her breakfast.

"Here you go," Bernie said as he set a tray holding a plate with two slices of toast cut into triangles, a glass pot of jam and a large mug of freshly brewed coffee. "Milk and sugar? Cream?"

"Just as it is. Thanks, Bernie." She placed her phone across from her and reached for the coffee. Bernie was about to walk away when she remembered to ask, "My Google search tells me there's a new mall in Bennington. Have you been? Is it very big?" She hated shopping for clothes but now her mission for the day was to purchase something more suitable to wear to Devon's dinner than the jeans and sweaters she'd brought.

"I haven't been, but I've heard via the Glen grapevine that it's not as big as those in larger cities, if that tells you anything."

"The Glen grapevine?" Now Bernie had her full attention.

"What the locals call the gossip mill in these parts. Jokingly of course, but—"

"With a hint of irony?"

"More like a hint of truth. Folks here aren't mean and nasty…the grapevine is all about interest and speculation. If you know what I mean."

Annika decided the grapevine could play a role in her first podcast episode. "And is there a particular source that generates all that interest and speculation?"

His expression shifted at that question and Annika realized she might have crossed a line with it.

"Who knows? Now, can I get you anything else?"

"Um, this is fine, Bernie. Thanks. Oh, one more question. How far is the Manor from here?"

He swung round, frowning. "You mean the McAllister place?"

"Yes. I've been invited for dinner tonight and wonder if I'll need to take my car."

"Heavens no. It's just a fifteen-minute walk from here, more or less, depending on your speed." He paused barely a second. "Are you family or…?"

Now it was Annika's turn to be cagey. "Um, kind of. More like…old friends." Her voice pitched in a question and his frown deepened.

"Uh, well, if you make a right when you go

out my front door and walk toward the forest marking the access to the Long Trail, you'll come to Otter Creek and a small footbridge. The Manor is on your left, just before the bridge. You can't miss it."

"Great. Thanks, Bernie. When will you need to know how long I'll be staying?"

"Checkout is eleven as you know, but I don't have many guests at the moment. One just checked out before you came down for breakfast. If you want to stay longer, you can let me know by late afternoon."

"I guess most tourists will come closer to Thanksgiving."

"For sure, but I do have a group that's coming just before Halloween. A club of some kind, exploring and investigating local paranormal occurrences. There've always been rumors of unexplained events here, as in other places, but nothing has ever been proven. For some reason these people think there's some truth to these stories."

"What do you think, as a longtime resident?"

"Lots of rural places have such tales and the Trail probably has more than most simply because it's a vast wilderness in parts and stretches through a few states. Personally, I think it's all nonsense."

"One of the stories I read focused on the children that were lost near Maple Glen and were eventually found by a local man." She was baiting him, hoping to get his take on Chloe and Billy Morrison.

His expression shifted again, as if a door had closed that Bernie didn't plan to reopen. "Hmm, best get back to the kitchen. I've got cinnamon rolls rising in the oven and if you come down earlier tomorrow morning, you might get one."

Interesting, thought Annika. The story about Chloe and Billy Morrison had headlined many newspapers so it wasn't exactly private, but the reports hadn't mentioned the names the children later assumed to escape public scrutiny—Devon and Dan Fairchild. Annika knew those names because their father, Blake Morrison, had also been her father. And she knew the name of the man who'd found the children. Walter Ingram.

Twenty-five years ago, he'd been a firefighter volunteer, one of many participating in the search for the missing children. Eventually the story faded from the media spotlight, and her research had failed to reveal anything current about the man either on social media or in any of the leading Vermont newspapers. She guessed he still lived in the area and bet that Devon remained in contact with him. He might be a good source of valley tales, especially since he himself was now part of recent lore. And if she was lucky, she might even get Devon to introduce her to him as a possible subject for the new podcast series on local legends and heroes that she hoped Venture Media would accept. The fact that she had a family connection to the story would be a bonus when making her pitch.

Annika downed the last of her coffee and got up to leave. She heard Bernie clattering in the kitchen and hollered a thank-you as she headed upstairs. Half an hour later she was on her way to the mall in Bennington. Once she turned onto Route 7 from Maple Glen's main street, Annika sped up. She wanted to get the shopping ordeal over with in good time because she hoped to edit her new pitch to Venture Media. Meanwhile, she'd begin to collect information about other local legends and a dinner party in Maple Glen might just be the best place to start.

The two-lane highway was busy with traffic and Annika realized many drivers were taking in the stunning fall colors all around them. She gritted her teeth, frustrated by the repeating flashes of brake lights as drivers slowed down, and once she'd angled her car enough to check that there was no oncoming vehicle, she moved out of her lane to pass the two cars ahead of her. She'd just returned to her own lane when she heard a horn blaring behind her. Checking her rearview mirror, she saw the car's headlights flashing and, worried that there might be something amiss with her rental car, pulled over onto the side of the road.

The car rolled up behind hers and Annika checked her rearview mirror, watching a man exit the car and head toward her. He wasn't wearing any kind of uniform, but there was something about him that was familiar. Not just his height and well-toned physique, but the way he strode with authority and purpose. A man comfortable with himself. Still, Annika locked her doors and when he tapped at her window, she lowered it just enough to speak. "Um, yes?"

"Yes, ma'am. I'm a new sheriff in Bennington County and clocked you going at least ten miles over the limit."

"You don't look like a sheriff and that's definitely not a cruiser." She eyed the brown Ford Fiesta behind him.

"Well, I'm not officially the new sheriff until next week."

"So you're a civilian right now?"

"Yes, ma'am, and passing on some advice that I sincerely hope you'll follow, especially after next week, keep to the speed limit."

"So, no ticket, then?"

A long pause, followed by an exasperated sigh. "Not this time. Where are you headed?"

"Um, Bennington."

"Okay, well I'll follow you for a bit to make sure you don't speed up again."

"If you insist," she said, flashing her best smile. A speeding ticket was the last thing her current finances needed. He kept his eyes on her a moment longer, as if trying to read her mind, she wondered? Then he gave a quick nod and returned to his car. When she saw him get inside, she clicked her turn signal, checked for traffic coming from behind and slowly crawled back onto the highway. Sure enough, he stayed on her tail until the Welcome to Bennington sign appeared on the side of the highway. Then he sped up, pulled into the other lane and passed her.

NATE'S MEETING WITH Sheriff Anderson in the low-rise county offices on the outskirts of Bennington didn't last long. The man wasn't well and clearly wanted to pass on the information quickly and leave. Nate felt bad for him, knowing his early retirement must be as difficult to process as his recently diagnosed illness.

"Yours is a new position in the county, as you knew when you applied for the job. Folks in Otter Valley, which includes parts of Bennington County and the village of Maple Glen, have been wanting their own law enforcement rather than relying on our team of sheriffs here in Bennington. As such, the position will be under review in a year's time and a decision made to keep the Valley Sheriff on as an independent office or to amalgamate it with Bennington Police Department. Until then, you will operate under the auspices of Bennington Police as I have, and the commander, Chief McNaught, will be your official superior and boss. Frankly, I don't know how this is all going to work. It's a bit of a hodgepodge as far as I'm concerned. My first question for you is, will either decision—permanent or interim—fit with your career plans?"

If only Nate knew what those plans might be. His decision to apply for the job had been based solely on the county's proximity to Maple Glen and Walter Ingram. He hadn't thought beyond that.

"Definitely, sir. I'm flexible when it comes to my future plans." He noted the other man's puzzled frown. "Big-city policing was challenging at times," he went on to say, choosing to omit the details behind his resignation.

"I can imagine. And just to warn you, your biggest challenge here might be to find enough police work to keep you busy. A lot of your time will be devoted to community liaison, and the success of that will determine the eventual outcome of a permanent position."

"Yes, sir, that was made clear in the application process."

"Okay, I'm just confirming your understanding. So, on to the job itself. As you know, it's basically a nine to five, Monday to Friday posting for the year. Your specific police station is located on Route 7 near the town of Wallingford, and a resident of Wallingford, Shelley Barnett, is the part-time dispatcher. She likes to go in early and leave a bit early, so as to be home when her kids finish school for the day. I've asked her to open up early Monday morning to meet you, give you a set of keys and so on. Any emergency situations in your station's off hours are automatically redirected to Bennington police station.

"Second, your best bet is to establish a good relationship with a local man, Finn McAllister. He's the county fire chief but he grew up in Maple Glen, and his family goes way back. He's a reliable and decent fellow who's not taken in by local gossip and such. Plus, he's highly respected, so if folks know you're working with him, they'll warm to you quicker. You'll be expected to liaise with residents in some capacity, either on a town or village council or a committee of some sort." He paused to take a breath.

Nate took in the man's shaky hands and pale complexion. He was about to suggest a break of some kind or to continue the next day when Anderson resumed speaking, obviously wanting to get on with things.

"Another piece of advice—if you can find accommodations right in the village of Maple Glen itself, they'll accept you even more. I never did that, and looking back, I think I might have cemented more of a bond with the valley residents."

Nate didn't mention he'd already heard of McAllister, first at the bakery and then inspecting the Shady Nook rooftop. He especially didn't mention his impulsive decision to stop a speeding car earlier that morning, knowing he'd overstepped boundaries there. He hadn't yet been sworn in and had no law enforcement status. He'd regretted the impulse all the way to his meeting and hoped the woman was long gone from Otter Valley. The enormous sunglasses she'd been wearing had done little to hide her beauty, magnified by a smile he bet was well practiced. Definitely not his kind of woman. That random thought begged the question, *then why are you still thinking about her, Gallagher?*

"And that's it," the sheriff said, rousing Nate from his daydreaming and signaling the end to the meeting. He wiped a hand across his forehead, heaved a long sigh and asked, "Any questions?"

Nate had a lot, jotted in a notebook that he'd left in his room at the B and B, but could recall a couple. "My cruiser?" An important detail he'd considered since stopping the woman who was speeding.

"It's being serviced and should be ready in a day or two. I usually decorate it and join the annual Halloween parade, but that'll be your call of course. Your status as interim carries all the weight of an elected officer, as you know, and once you've been sworn in, you're good to go."

Right. His other question. "Where and when does that happen?"

"Either in Bennington at the courthouse or even here. I'll be happy to set it up for you. You can either go there for it, or I can request a travelling justice to come here, but that might take longer."

Nate saw his anticipated free days of being a civilian vanish but figured he'd already learned plenty about Maple Glen. "I'm happy to go there, sir."

"Fine. I can organize that for you. By the way, you may be able to pick up your uniforms at the same time. A clerk there will direct you where to go. I assume you sent your measurements with your acceptance email?"

"Yes, sir, I did."

"And has Finn McAllister contacted you yet? I left a phone message with him yesterday that you'd arrived."

"No, but I'm sure he's a busy man heading up the only fire department in the county."

"True, and I'll send him a reminder. Soon enough you'll be a busy man yourself, as the only law enforcement in Otter Valley."

Busy ticketing illegally parked cars, Nate thought, recalling Bernie Watson's comment yesterday. However, policing in the valley would definitely be a healthy break from Boston and that thought raised a question he needed to ask. "Um, are there any current law enforcement issues here that I ought to know about, sir?"

"Law enforcement issues here? Not so far," he said, shaking his head and shrugging at the same time.

Nate was reassured by the incredulity in the man's response and didn't pursue his point. He'd find out for himself soon enough. He simply nodded and stood up to leave.

"Good luck with your new post, Officer Gallagher, and I'll advise you of your swearing-in as soon as I know myself. Oh, and one last thing, you officially won't be able to drive the cruiser until that happens. I assume you have your own set of wheels here?"

"I do, sir."

"After you've been sworn in, claim any expenses you accrued getting here on your sheriff's account. The amount varies from election to election, but I still have a respectable balance in the budget that should get you through until after the next election, in a year's time. You'll need to use it for any office purchases and so on."

Nate heard a stifled groan as Sheriff Anderson leaned back in his swivel chair. He was tired already and probably looking forward to going home. "If you contact the courthouse in Bennington today, someone there might be able to expedite my swearing-in," Nate suggested.

"Good idea, especially as today's Thursday and otherwise you might have to wait until after the weekend. A little pressure often works with administrative people, and I might as well use what I can while I'm still sheriff. I'll let you know as soon as I find out." He stood up and held out his hand. "Good luck with your new post, Officer Gallagher."

Nate was on his way to the parking lot when he got the text from Finn McAllister inviting him to dinner that night at the Manor.

Casual. Meet my family and maybe a few community residents.

Nate grimaced. Okay, get used to it, he told himself, recalling Sheriff Anderson's advice about establishing and maintaining contacts with the county residents. He figured community involvement might include social events, which he'd avoided as much as possible in Boston. But he wanted to learn his family history, perhaps even meet his biological father, and working in Maple Glen could accomplish those goals.

CHAPTER THREE

HER EYES WERE the giveaway and the flaming-red hair, the clincher. When Finn introduced her as Devon's half-sister, Nate already knew two things about Annika Morrison. First, that she was the Shady Nook guest who'd made free use of his telescope last night to spy on the very people who were hosting the dinner party. *Her family.* Second, he was pretty certain she was the woman wearing large sunglasses whom he'd clocked for speeding that morning, and who definitely hadn't left Maple Glen for good, as he'd hoped.

He didn't quite know what to make of those two facts, but his sleuthing instincts were on high alert. He noted that she, too, recognized him from the stop on Route 7 and the expression in her bright blue eyes wasn't imploring him not to say anything so much as daring him to. He was intrigued and a bit puzzled. Most people would simply laugh and say something like, "Oops, I think we've already met," though to be honest, Nate wasn't that kind of person anyway and clearly, neither was she. So, he decided to go along with her and when Finn mentioned that Nate would soon be the new Bennington County sheriff, Nate kept his eyes fixed on hers.

When she replied, "Soon?" with a slight arch of an eyebrow, Nate resisted the urge to laugh, because he didn't want to give her even the slightest edge in this game they were playing. The moment was interrupted by the arrival of more guests, and Nate found himself being guided around the living room by Finn to meet other Maple Glen residents. All the while he kept scanning the group for an older man who could be Walter Ingram, but most everyone seemed to be in his own age range—mid to late thirties.

There was Maura Stuart who invited him to ride the donkeys at Jake & Friends riding stables. Nate decided he'd give the actual riding a pass but smiled politely and said he would like to visit. Theo Danby, Maura's doctor husband, advised Nate that the medical clinic in Wallingford had recently hired a new doctor if Nate ever needed one and Nate mentally crossed his fingers, but thanked the man. Then he wondered if the clinic provided DNA tests and immediately decided he was getting way too far ahead of himself. He had yet to meet Ingram, and what if he didn't even like the man? In that case he'd prefer not knowing any DNA results at all.

"Have you met everyone yet, Nate?"

Startled, he glanced to his left and down to a pretty, dark-haired woman. "I'm Devon, Finn's fiancée, and so happy that you could make it tonight on such short notice. Finn wasn't expecting you in the Glen until next week."

"Very pleased to meet you, Devon. I've met a few people but perhaps not everyone. And yes, my actual tenure as sheriff in the county doesn't begin until I'm sworn in. I wanted to come a bit earlier to check out the place and find accommodations."

"Maybe Finn and I can help you with that. Some friends of ours, Will and Leni Bower, have just moved into a new home and they've been trying to sublet their old one, but there aren't a lot of potential renters here in the Glen."

"That would be great. The B and B is nice, but obviously I'll need something for at least a year."

"I've invited them tonight and perhaps you'll get a chance to inquire about the house. Finn and I didn't want to make this evening seem like a business affair, so we've only asked friends. I'm sure the council in Bennington will organize a meet-and-greet with elected politicians and local merchants."

"No doubt that might happen after my official swearing-in."

"When will that be?"

"Soon. I think Sheriff Anderson is ready to leave his post."

"From what I've gathered through the local gossip mill, people are happy to have a younger sheriff who'll be more involved with the community."

"Gossip mill?"

"People here call it the Glen grapevine. You're going to hear that expression a lot."

"Thanks for the heads-up. Or is that a warning?"

She smiled. "Both, but as I said, folks here are generally welcoming, so no need to worry about it."

"I'm usually not the worrying kind, Devon. I like to see how things play out before making decisions."

"Good traits for a police officer, I should think."

Nate silently agreed but thought maybe not so great for a social life. He noticed Finn waving to Devon from across the room. "Um, I think you're being paged."

She craned her head. "Yup, time to eat I'm guessing." She moved to the center of the room and clapped her hands. "Dinner is ready folks, and I hope you're hungry because Finn has barbecued a heap of steaks and ribs. Sit wherever you like in the dining room across the hall."

Nate counted sixteen places at the long dining table and waited until most people were seated before pulling out the chair between Maura Stuart and a woman who introduced herself as Leni Bower.

"Have you got everyone's names sorted out yet?" she quipped.

"Working on it," Nate admitted. "But I've met your husband—" he tilted his head to his left, across the table "—and he's invited me to tour your maple syrup shed. Though from what I saw on my drive into Maple Glen, that building isn't exactly a shed."

"No, it isn't. But Will's a traditionalist and likes to call it that. When you come for the tour, pop into my farm shop next door to the shed."

"Farm shop? I like the sound of that. What can I buy there?"

"Lots of yummy food things, some handmade items like potholders, tea towels and tablecloths, plus preserves from Devon's mother-in-law and of course, our own family's maple syrup. Oh, and there's honey, too, from Walter."

The name was bound to come up, but still Nate tensed. "Walter?" he asked as casually as he could.

"Walter Ingram. He's a beekeeper and has a small operation, providing honey to some local merchants—like me—and sometimes he sells to people who just drop in to see the place."

"Um, he's not here tonight though?"

She gave a light laugh. "Not Walter. He's a bit of a hermit when it comes to socializing, though we think that might soon be changing."

"Oh?" Nate said, trying not to seem too interested.

"He's been seeing a woman about the same age."

"The Glen grapevine at work, I assume?"

"Caught me there," she said sheepishly.

Nate decided it was time to shift topics. "I'm looking for accommodations and Devon told me you and your husband might have a house to rent."

"We do! It was my childhood home, and eventually it'll be torn down to enlarge the parking area for the farm shop. Will and I have recently moved into a new house on the far side of the property. There's plenty of space between the two houses that our children shouldn't bother you, but I can't guarantee there won't be the occasional shouts and laughter of kids at play."

A welcome change from the sound of traffic and police sirens, Nate thought. "So, you have children."

"I have a son and a daughter from my previous marriage and will be eternally grateful that they and Will have made a connection. A very special connection," she explained.

Nate saw her glance across the table at Will, her eyes tearing up. She reached for her glass of water and took a long sip. While he waited, knowing she needed the moment, he thought about his stepfather, Paul. They'd had a connection too, but he'd been ten when Paul and his mother married and thirteen when they'd divorced.

He was drawn out of the memory when she added, "The house is fully furnished and you're welcome to use everything plus perhaps even take some things when you find permanent living quarters. I'll get Will to text you tomorrow and you can drop by the farm shop for a key."

"Thank you," Nate said. He hoped his stay in Maple Glen wouldn't be longer than a year, but appreciated the offer along with the hospitality he'd received so far.

Further conversation with Leni was curtailed by the arrival of platters of barbecued meats and bowls of vegetables. Devon and Finn took their own places at either end of the long dining table while their guests exclaimed over the food. Nate dug in, but couldn't resist occasional glances to his left, across the table.

He noticed that Devon's sister—half-sister, he corrected himself—didn't seem as hungry as the others. She toyed with the food and barely spoke to the people on either side—Theo, the doctor, and Matt somebody who was also a firefighter at Finn's station. He wondered what she was thinking and then immediately recalled the promise he'd made to himself when he took the job as interim sheriff. Once he was sworn in, perceptions, not to mention relationships, could and probably would, change, which was why he'd need to avoid any personal involvements that might conflict with his work.

Soon people were putting on coats and saying their goodbyes at the front door. Maura and Theo offered Nate a drive to the B and B, which he politely declined. As he strode down the driveway to Maple Glen's main street—Church Street, he recalled—he was aware of footsteps from behind. He swung around and saw Devon's sister, Annika, following him. Or seeming to, though she was scrolling through a cell phone. Nate sighed. Another one of his pet peeves. They really had little in common, and then he frowned. *What does it matter, Gallagher?*

He slowed down and still focusing on her phone, she almost bumped into him. "I think we're both heading the same way," he said as she came to an abrupt stop inches away from him.

"Um, yes."

She sounded a tad wary, Nate thought. Maybe worried that he might raise the speeding incident or even last night's encounter on the roof of the Shady Nook? He tried to set her at ease. "Will you be staying long in Maple Glen?"

The question had the opposite effect. "Why do you ask?"

Nate bit his lip. For some reason he and this woman seemed destined to misunderstand each other. "No particular reason." He paused to add, "Small talk isn't my thing, I'm afraid." Her light laugh was unexpected.

"Same here." She looked up at him, her eyes reflecting the amber glow of the streetlight behind Nate. "At least we have that in common."

"It's a start."

Her slightly snorted laugh brought Nate back to his senses, as he realized his blurted comment sounded like flirting. He needed to get back onto a neutral path at once. "I mean—"

"It's okay, Sheriff Gallagher. I know what you meant." Her smile disappeared, but she kept her eyes on his. "Given the size of Maple Glen, I'm certain we will encounter one another on more than a few occasions, so I suggest that we begin our first real introductions here, right now."

Nate looked down at her right hand, extended for a handshake, and took hold of it. Despite the chilly night, her hand was warm and soft. His mind drifted for a split second until he caught her grinning up at him and he let go.

"I'm Annika Morrison, as you know, and Devon's half-sister. I'm from New Hampshire and came here to meet her and her family. I'm a podcaster and I'm planning to write a series of podcasts about folklore and legends in Vermont. Particularly, in small towns like Maple Glen."

Nate took a minute to sift through the flood of information, but one item got his attention. Podcast. "Um, then you'll be interviewing people here for their stories?"

"You got it," she quipped.

He immediately thought of Walter Ingram and the option of meeting him in a neutral situation with another person on hand. "Maybe we can work together a bit. Sort of a collaboration."

She took her time replying. "Maybe we can, Sheriff Gallagher. Let's meet up tomorrow and talk."

"Sure," he said, though now he was regretting the blurted suggestion. Was it wise to work with someone he hardly knew on as potentially a sensitive topic as the personal stories of Maple Glen residents? The very people he'd soon be policing? He decided right then to backtrack on his offer to work with her but would let her know, perhaps the next day, by text or email. He realized procrastinating wasn't ideal but couldn't bring himself to disappoint her in person and see that bright smile fade.

They resumed walking but seconds later, she asked in a lilting voice, "So, what's your story, Sheriff?"

She really liked to tease, Nate was thinking. Yet there was an edge to her, and he wondered if the light humor and teasing were a facade, hiding something more serious. He liked a good mystery, and maybe here was one to solve.

"Nothing very glamorous, much less interesting, I'm afraid," he replied.

"Hmm, I think you're doing yourself an injustice, Sheriff Gallagher. Tell me what's captured your interest up there—" she pointed to the night sky "—enough to bring a telescope to Maple Glen."

And so Nate began to tell her about the Fireworks Galaxy and how his mother bought him a telescope for his twelfth birthday. He was still talking when they reached the front door of the B and B.

"Will you show it to me sometime?"

"Okay, but on a clear night." Nate had no idea where or when the conversation shifted from small talk to a topic as important as stargazing, but he felt a stir of both excitement and trepidation as he opened the door for this beautiful but enigmatic woman.

SHERIFF GALLAGHER WAS CUTE. *No, you're not a teenager, Morrison.* Cute wasn't the right word at all. Handsome, in an old-fashioned kind of way. The hawkish nose and the lines at the edges of his dark brown eyes were the hallmarks of someone who'd seen too much of the world. She wondered if he'd find being sheriff in Bennington County a tad dull but figured his job policing in Boston had etched many of those lines and perhaps he'd welcome the change of pace.

At any rate, you won't be around long enough to learn the answer to that, Morrison, so best get on with your new podcast project; and if getting to know Sheriff Gallagher, and through him more people in the valley, speeds up that process, so be it. Achieving that goal with an attractive sheriff as partner is an even better proposition.

She put the finishing touches to her ponytail, going for a casual look that was somewhat negated by eyeliner and a dab of lipstick. Satisfied with the overall result reflected back in her room mirror, she headed downstairs for breakfast. The Shady Nook dining room was empty and all the tables cleared except for one. Annika sighed. She'd missed him and hadn't received a text regarding their tentative meeting. Maybe he'd changed his mind.

Bernie popped his head in from the kitchen doorway. "The usual?"

"Yes, please. Thanks, Bernie."

He almost seemed disappointed, but she'd never been a breakfast person, not even as a growing teenager. She wondered if he had lots of leftovers and then imagined Nate Gallagher wolfing down a full breakfast. *Back to the sheriff again, Morrison?*

As Bernie was setting down her coffee—black, no sugar—she asked, "Is business slower than usual, Bernie? Just that I'd have thought there'd be a lot of tourists coming for the fall colors."

"Those tourists come and go throughout the valley, but many don't make it as far as Maple Glen, unless they're hikers wanting to access the Long Trail here."

"I'm sure they'd have to be skilled or at least very competent hikers to tackle the Trail from here."

"It would help, to be sure, but as long as folks stay on the path and follow the blazes, they should be okay. Hiking at the right time of year helps, too."

He lapsed into a thoughtful silence and Annika wondered if he was thinking of her half-sister who set out on a winter's day almost a year ago. Devon had been lucky that she hadn't seriously injured herself when she'd fallen on an ice-covered piece of slate, and luckier still that the person who found her had been a search and rescue volunteer who knew what he was doing. Now that rescuer—Finn McAllister—was marrying Devon after a head-spinning courtship. Annika felt a slight twinge of envy, even though she knew she wasn't the romantic type at all.

"Have you decided how long you'll want to keep the room?" Bernie asked.

Annika thought of her dwindling bank account and Devon's repeated offer last night. Although the B and B was a neutral place, she figured she'd get more inside information on the day-to-day business of Maple Glen along with some facts behind the grapevine rumors by staying with Devon and family. All fodder for the podcast she hoped to pitch to Venture Media when they replied to the email query she'd sent that morning.

"Actually, I'll be moving over to the Manor today." She saw that he was struggling not to yield to his curiosity and decided he'd find out some of the story soon enough.

"Devon is my half-sister. We shared the same father, who passed away years ago."

"Oh, my goodness! That's quite an ending to a famous story. You two getting together, I mean."

Yes, it was, Annika was thinking, and the story was nowhere finished yet.

CHAPTER FOUR

NATE ARRIVED IN Bennington half an hour before his meeting with the county justice to be sworn in as the new interim sheriff of Otter Valley. He'd received the text from Sheriff Anderson as he was finishing breakfast at the B and B and considered leaving a note to tell Annika Morrison that they'd have to schedule their meeting for another time, but in the end, he decided to tell her when he saw her next that he couldn't collaborate with her. Annika seemed like the type to stir things up, and distancing himself from her would be prudent. So, he hadn't kept the vague promise to meet with her, nor had he even left a message, and he felt bad about that, but figured she'd get the information she needed for her podcast all on her own.

The two-story district courthouse was an unimposing structure located in the north end of town. Nate pulled into the parking lot and killed time by scrolling through his cell phone. He was still in contact with some of his former colleagues in Boston but knew from experience that those links would eventually vanish. His once-upon-a-time romance with a workmate had dissolved more than a year ago and Nate had no interest in looking for a replacement.

Negative messages from former colleagues about the incoming police chief confirmed his decision to resign. Nate was looking forward to being his own boss for a change, although he knew he'd have to prove himself to a committee of Maple Glen residents and the Bennington County Council until the election in a year's time, when he'd find out if the interim position would become a permanent one. Until then, he'd sit on the proverbial fence as much as possible when it came to handling opposing community viewpoints. Professionally, that was the best stance to take as working in Boston had taught him. And personally, he might have more success learning about Walter Ingram if no one knew about their family connection.

He noted the time and got out of his car to head into the courthouse. The whole swearing-in took less than five minutes and a few handshakes later Nate was on his way back to Maple Glen. He'd been told to pick up his cruiser at Bennington police headquarters in a couple of days along with his two sets of uniforms. He stopped for a coffee at the convenience store and gas station on Route 7 outside Maple Glen and texted Finn that he was now officially Sheriff Gallagher until the local elections in a year. Then he texted Will and Leni Bower to say that he appreciated their offer of a rental house and would take them up on it. He received an instant one-line reply—the door's unlocked, go right on in—and smiled, thinking again how hospitality in the village was a given. He hoped the trust people had in each other here would never be shaken.

When he arrived back at the B and B to collect his luggage, he met Bernie exiting the front door.

"Just going to the bakery," Bernie explained. "Have you decided to stay on or…?"

"I'm checking out, Bernie. Going to be moving into Leni Bower's former home for my stay here, so I'll need to square things up with you."

"You can pay me what you owe me later. I know where you'll be."

Nate smiled at his wink. "Fair enough. If you text me the amount I can e-transfer it to you."

"Nah, I prefer cash, credit card or a check," he said, waving a dismissive hand. "Whenever it suits you."

Definitely not Boston, Nate thought as he continued on upstairs to pack. As he reached the second floor, he noticed three of the six rooms had opened doors and a large utility cart sat outside one of them. The day's checkouts, Nate wondered, or simply rooms being cleaned? Had one of them been Annika's? He walked across to the stairs leading to his room on the third floor, trying not to nosily peer through the open doorways. She'd probably moved to the Manor, and he felt a sense of relief that at least there'd be some distance between them—as much as Maple Glen allowed, that is.

Traveling light meant packing up was quick and easy. If the interim placement became permanent and he did decide to stay, he'd have the rest of his belongings shipped. Once he stowed everything in his car, he drove out of the B and B parking lot onto Church Street and headed toward the end of Maple Glen close to Route 7, where the Bowers lived. When he saw the roof of the maple syrup shed, he began to slow down. Will had texted that the driveway wasn't easy to spot from the road, but that it was to the right of the shed. More like warehouse, Nate thought again, as the large, aluminum-clad building came into view. A sign at the entrance to the place read Our Family's Maple Syrup and Farm Shop. Sure enough, as Will had warned, a turnoff almost concealed by trees appeared just before he reached the sign.

Nate signaled, though no other vehicles were in sight, and headed up the paved driveway to a two-story house that was unassuming in appearance except for the large building looming behind it. The farm shop, he figured. The driveway forked at the house, one part continuing on to the farm shop and the other curving to the front door. Nate pulled up there and turned off the engine. According to Leni, the house was destined to be torn down and replaced by a larger parking lot—all dependent on the success of her farm shop. Judging by the number of cars already in the current lot at nine in the morning, Nate guessed the house wasn't going to be standing long. He was beginning to realize that should his job become a permanent one, he might have to move to nearby Wallingford, rather than live in Maple Glen. A shame, he thought, because the picturesque village was beginning to soothe his big-city policing stresses.

The front door was unlocked, as Will had texted, and Nate stood for a moment in the entry hall, taking in the old-fashioned charms as well as the slight fustiness of a place that hadn't been inhabited for a while. Nothing that a good airing wouldn't cure, he told himself and then grinned. Exactly what his mother would have said. It wasn't long before he had his luggage and telescope unloaded and hauled upstairs, windows opened to let in the brisk autumn breeze and a decision made about which bedroom he'd use as his own. Not the master with its four-poster bed and a mattress that visibly sagged in the center, or the middle bedroom with a single window facing east, but the smaller room at the very back of the house with two windows that overlooked the acreage of maple trees and part of the warehouse to the west, and fields to the east.

Leni had told him the house had been her childhood home and was taken over by her and her two children before she married Will. Someone at the dinner party—he couldn't recall who—had mentioned Will's original childhood home had been knocked down to plant more maple trees for his business, plus the warehouse construction. Picturing the original layout of the properties, Nate wondered if a crush had developed between the two teens living side by side. If so, he thought their eventual marriage only months ago must have been the storybook culmination of some adolescent fantasies. He liked the idea that once upon a time they might have stared longingly out their windows at each other's house.

His view from the back room also included the Bower family's newly constructed home to the east. If he squinted, he could make out the end of Maple Glen at Otter Creek and the entrance to the Long Trail on that side. The peaks of the Green Mountains were barely visible through clouds rolling in and Nate figured a change in the weather was imminent. But perhaps these signs were simply part of the weather vagaries in the valley. He smiled. Soon enough he could be speaking like a valley old-timer. The idea amused him, though he doubted he'd be around long enough to earn that moniker. Once he made some kind of contact with Walter Ingram—and he had yet to determine how and when that would occur—he'd know if he wanted to stay in Maple Glen.

Right now, he had a job to commit to, and the length of his tenure was predicated on how well he fulfilled his duties as sheriff and also, on whether he even wanted a permanent position, given that he had yet to learn much about the community he was going to serve. The option to leave after one year was the condition that meant the most to him. There was no way he was going to be trapped in another job situation like the one he'd left behind in Boston.

He unpacked and decided to drive to Wallingford to buy groceries and any other items he'd need, though a cursory search through kitchen cupboards and drawers revealed plenty of gadgets, more than he'd ever use, since meal preparation had never been of interest to him. There was an old-model microwave on one counter, so he'd manage just fine.

After he locked up—deciding he wasn't yet ready to take on Maple Glen's open-door policy—he received a text from outgoing Sheriff Anderson telling him his cruiser would be ready earlier for pickup—the next day, Saturday—and his uniforms a few days later. Now everyone in the valley would definitely be aware of his comings and goings and any hope of anonymity would be gone. Nate could live with that, but he felt a small twinge of regret that distancing himself from Annika Morrison meant he might not get to tell her all about the Fireworks Galaxy. And that was just as well too, considering the spark inside him whenever she was nearby.

ANNIKA APPRECIATED THE loan of the stone cottage behind Devon and Finn's home but her first impression—small and rustic—had her doubting the wisdom of staying in Maple Glen until the wedding at Thanksgiving. There was a fireplace and a newly installed woodstove in the large open-plan living area that Finn proclaimed would heat the whole place, but otherwise no furnace or even electric baseboard heating. The bathroom had a clawfoot bathtub that Annika figured some wealthy city type might pay big bucks for, but no shower. Her loud sigh echoed in the largest of the two bedrooms where she began to unpack.

On the plus side, there was plenty of privacy as the cottage was well behind the Manor, at the end of a gravel lane leading directly from Maple Glen's main throughfare, Church Street. She liked the idea that she could come and go without drawing too much attention, something she figured would be an asset in Maple Glen, and was glad she'd decided to keep her rental car until she knew how long she'd be staying in the village. So much depended on her success selling the new podcast idea!

The cottage itself was well equipped and fortunately there was a microwave. She'd also found a coffee bean grinder that had seen better days but would ensure a daily fresh cup. The place had internet connection because Finn's mother had been living in it prior to moving to Wallingford to be with her daughter, Roxanne, and granddaughter, Kaya. Annika knew some of the story behind Devon's fall on the Long Trail and her rescue by Finn McAllister last Christmas. She'd thought that story would make a great podcast episode, but her half-sister was a very private person and would probably hate the idea.

Eventually though, other ideas for episodes would come to her, especially now that she was living in a place fueled by a gossip mill. The Glen grapevine would be the perfect title of a podcast episode, assuming she could connect

Maple Glen to stories about the Appalachian Trail. She'd almost finished the first episode for her potential new series on local legends and folklore— a tale about Lake Champlain, nearby, and its legendary underwater creature named Champy. Her online research had revealed that the comical character was the focus of many summer community events in that part of Vermont, and she thought listeners would be amused and interested. But she hoped to find stories that were more suspenseful and mysterious, drawing in a wider audience.

Halloween was approaching and Annika decided some local spooky tales would enhance her pitch to Venture Media. She'd received a reply to her email about the new series idea from her contact at Venture, Christine Henderson, who had shown some interest, with the added caveat "the sooner the better" as she was making up a new airing schedule.

Once she was unpacked, she decided to drive into Wallingford to buy some supplies. As she passed the Manor, she noted that a couple of cars were parked behind Devon's SUV in the driveway. Annika caught herself wondering who her half-sister was entertaining and immediately grinned. *Oh yes, you're definitely getting into small-town vibes!*

She kept an eye on the car's speedometer as

she drove along Church Street to the junction of Route 7, reluctant to encounter Sheriff Gallagher again, although the idea intrigued her. Would he issue her a ticket this time around, or let her off the hook now that they had mutual acquaintances in Maple Glen? No, she decided. He seemed the type to follow rules, and she was the opposite. Not necessarily a rule breaker, but definitely a rule challenger.

What did those differences portend for a collaboration with the man? Not promising, Annika thought. Plus, the fact that he'd left the B and B without any word about their planned meeting grated. She wasn't used to being stood up and her first instinct was to contact him and let him know how she felt. Except she didn't have a cell phone number or even an email address. Not that she'd need that information. Given the size of Maple Glen, she'd have the opportunity sooner or later to vent her feelings in person.

There was a single grocery store in Wallingford. It didn't qualify as a supermarket and only offered the basic items people might need rather than having to drive to Bennington or Burlington. Annika wandered the four aisles, scanning shelves half-heartedly. The freezer section offered a modest selection of ice cream and her spirits picked up. At least there'd be dessert. She plunked two cartons—strawberry and chocolate—into her basket then rounded an aisle to look for frozen microwaveable meals. If she had to cook for herself, there was a small array of fresh vegetables, meat and fruit, but the choices were limited, and she realized at some point she'd need to shop at a larger outlet. She was making her way to one of the two checkout counters when she heard a male voice behind her.

"I suppose meeting at the only grocery store close to Maple Glen was inevitable."

Annika swung around, the wire basket she was holding bumping against the basket in Nate Gallagher's hands. "I was stood up for grocery shopping?" Her voice pitched.

"Sorry about that. I can explain."

She noted his red face. "Just teasing, Sheriff," and recalling the email she'd just sent to Venture Media, she added, "Over a cup of coffee?"

"Um, okay."

Ignoring the reluctance in his tone, she said, "Come to my place then, because I have to take care of these frozen products." She caught his slight smile when he looked down into her basket. "Not into cooking," she explained.

"Yep, same here."

She saw that his own shopping extended to instant noodle soup cups, salsa and corn tortilla chips. "I think a quick stop at the bakery will be next then, and just to reassure you, I make a good cup of coffee."

"Sounds like a plan."

He sounded resigned, rather than pleased. As Annika's groceries were scanned, she resisted looking behind at him, not wanting to catch any facial expression that would make her feel bad about putting him on the spot. Still, she rationalized, *He stood you up, not the other way around.*

Less than an hour later, Annika spotted Nate's car pulling up in front of the cottage and she turned on the coffee machine. When she opened the front door, she thought he didn't look any happier about meeting with her than he had at the grocery store but hoped she could change his mood with a good cup of coffee.

He took off his baseball cap as he walked inside and paused to take in the large stone wall on one side of the cottage and the stained wood on the other three walls. The furnishings—a three-seater sofa and a couple of reclining chairs—were fairly new, but the lamps and small tables at either end of the sofa looked like antiques. At least Annika thought they might be, though old furniture wasn't her style.

Nate, on the other hand, seemed entranced by them, walking over to each piece and staring for a few seconds, while Annika suppressed a grin.

"How do you take your coffee?" she asked,

and he blinked, as if he had just tuned in to her presence.

"Um, black."

"Perfect." She headed for the galley kitchen at the far end of the big room. It had been modernized, probably prior to Finn's mother moving in. Annika supposed she'd meet the rest of Finn's family before the wedding at Thanksgiving.

She and Devon had grown up separately. Devon, in the foster care system along with her now-deceased brother, Dan, while Annika had two parents—the father whom she had shared with Devon and Dan—and her mother, Anna, who was still living in New Hampshire. The discovery of Blake Morrison's other children had upended the life Annika and her mother had made for themselves. Blake had never revealed to them that he'd had two children from a previous marriage and had died before he had a chance to reconnect with them. A bureaucratic mistake had resulted in his two young children being placed in foster care. After Dan passed away, Devon came to Maple Glen to carry out their plan to revisit the place where their new life had begun, twenty-five years earlier.

Sometimes Annika thought about how wonderful it might have been to know her half-brother, too, but fate had determined otherwise.

"Can I help?"

She almost jumped and realized she was staring at the coffee maker which had almost finished its cycle. Nate was standing slightly behind and to her left. He must have seen something in her face because his next question was, "Everything okay?"

"Yes," she blurted a bit more vehemently than she'd intended. "Just thinking about other people who've lived here in this cottage."

"It's an interesting place all right. What do you know about its history?"

"Not too much, but I think this is the original family home and the McAllisters simply kept it, even after the Manor was built."

"I think you're probably right." He peered around the room again. "I bet it didn't have a kitchen at all. Way back then, even grand houses, as this would have been at the time, had kitchens that were attached at the rear, like an annex, where fireplace cooking would have been done."

Annika stared at him, noticing for the first time how his brown eyes gleamed when he was talking about something he clearly felt a passion for. She watched his hands with their long, slender fingers stroking the polished wood of the old kitchen table, as if he were communicating with it, and her next thought instantly shifted to the thought of those fingers gently brushing up the side of her neck. She shivered.

He seemed to be suddenly aware of her focused attention. "In case of fire," he said, lowering his voice. "From cooking…so the house itself wouldn't burn down, too."

His face was inches away from hers. Close enough for a kiss. He leaned in and she held her breath. Then the coffee maker beeped and they drew apart.

"That was close," Annika said, with a light gasp.

His sigh echoed around the room and settled down on her as she saw a mix of disappointment and relief in his face. "Yes, uh, sorry about that Annika. I wasn't—"

"Thinking?"

"Exactly. Look, maybe we should rethink working together on your project…"

"You don't have to spell it out for me," she said. He raised his hands as if in surrender which annoyed her even more. She took a long, calming breath. "We're both well past those days, Nate. You know, the instant attraction and follow-up scenarios. I think we can put this moment behind us and get on with business. So…coffee?"

"Please."

She turned away from the intensity of his gaze. Was he looking for signs to navigate his way through the minefields of emotion that had suddenly appeared between them, she wondered?

The coffee maker emitted another, almost impatient beep and she felt a whoosh of relief mixed with disappointment as she lifted the pot and heard a tap on the front door.

"Can you get that?" she asked without turning around.

Voices got her attention then, and she set the coffee pot back down. Nate was standing in the open doorway and, although Annika couldn't see her, she heard Devon speaking.

"Hello, you two," her sister said, grinning. "I'm glad I caught you both at the same time. Some friends and I were meeting to discuss plans for the community center's Halloween events, and someone suggested the new sheriff might want to follow tradition with a decorated cruiser in the parade. Then someone else had another idea and thought Sheriff Gallagher would be a good addition to the Halloween planning committee itself."

Annika resisted glancing at Nate but felt a small rise of amusement, thinking participating in a parade might be the last thing he'd be interested in. But he surprised her.

"Definitely," Nate said. "I've already made the arrangement with Sheriff Anderson about decorating the cruiser. And I'm sure Annika and

I would be happy to be part of any Halloween planning," he said, flashing a quick grin at Annika.

"Maybe you could even write a podcast about the event, Annika," Devon suggested.

Annika fixed a light smile on her face and said, "Of course." Writing about Maple Glen's Halloween events would be the very last item on her list of podcast themes, but another furtive glance at Nate told her that this unexpected opportunity was a perfect excuse for spending more time with Sheriff Gallagher. And she had no intention of letting the chance slip away.

CHAPTER FIVE

NATE'S SATURDAY BEGAN with two text messages. The first from Sheriff Anderson telling him his cruiser was ready for pickup at the Bennington police station and also wishing him good luck on his new job. The man had already expressed his best wishes when Nate met him the other day, and for a second Nate questioned such a profuse goodbye from someone he hardly knew. But then he figured maybe this was a hallmark of small-town life—acquaintances becoming fast friends almost overnight. The dinner party at the Manor had felt like that. He knew he was analyzing the whole thing from the viewpoint of a big-city dweller, and a police officer to boot, so made an effort to temper his thoughts. The second text was from Finn McAllister informing Nate that the Bennington County Council was organizing a meet-and-greet for the county's new sheriff and hoped to have it at the community center in Maple Glen the next day, Sunday, if that suited Nate.

No, he thought. That didn't suit him at all, and he'd rather take a pass, but then he recalled Anderson's advice that knowing the community he served would make his job easier and perhaps more enjoyable. Nate doubted the latter, envisioning days spent ticketing illegally parked cars or setting up speed traps along Route 7 to catch the occasional fast driver. The image of Annika Morrison's brilliant smile popped into his head.

He texted a thank-you to Anderson and was about to reply to Finn when he had an idea. Perhaps Finn could combine Nate's introduction to residents with a meeting about general issues in the county and particularly, Maple Glen. That way Nate could save himself another community gathering. He'd participated in many such discussions in Boston, though on a larger scale, and sometimes found them to be counterproductive, often serving as an opportunity for people with an axe to grind or a vested interest in certain issues, especially where money was involved. He took his time phrasing his message, reluctant to have Finn take his suggestion the wrong way, because he needed to have someone like Finn on his side while he navigated the various, and possibly conflicting, opinions and moods of people in Maple Glen.

After he hit Send, he realized he'd need a ride to Bennington because he'd be driving the cruiser back to Maple Glen and could have asked Finn if he was available. On the other hand, the man was already going out of his way to assist Nate with his transition to Maple Glen. The next name that came to mind was Annika Morrison, who had her rental car, but he'd decided overnight that he should minimize any future contact with her, as much as anyone could avoid another person in Maple Glen. Yet there seemed to be no other choice.

Their meeting yesterday to discuss her podcast idea had fizzled out after Devon's arrival. Nate was relieved he'd reconsidered collaborating with her. That whole Glen grapevine thing was enough of a deterrent and Nate wanted—needed—to be in control of any situation that might jeopardize his job. There was too much at stake for him. His sole reason for taking the interim sheriff job here was to learn as much about Walter Ingram as possible before deciding next steps, and whether to reveal his connection to Ingram or not.

He was deliberating whether to go with Annika or not when his cell phone pealed. The unidentified caller banner would normally lead Nate to dismiss, delete or block, but he took a chance and picked up, almost relieved to hear Annika's voice.

"Hi, Nate, um Finn gave me your phone number and…uh… I plan to return my rental car today because Devon said I could use hers whenever I needed a car, and so I was wondering if you could follow me to Bennington to give me a ride back to Maple Glen because both Finn and Devon are busy."

Nate took a few seconds to process what she'd said, and his delay prompted her to add, "But if you're busy too, I can try to get an Uber ride though not sure about one coming all the way to Maple Glen."

"As it turns out my cruiser is ready for pickup in Bennington. You can drive my car back."

"Are you okay with that? Me driving your car, I mean?"

"Well, I'll be following you in my cruiser so—"

"No speeding."

"Nope." He heard her sharp intake of breath and wondered if she was stifling a laugh, or maybe a retort.

"I promise, Sheriff Gallagher."

There was a tease in her voice and Nate was beginning to realize his vow to maintain a professional relationship with her might be more difficult to keep than he'd thought.

"Okay then. I'm ready to leave now. We can return your rental first, then drive to the station to pick up my cruiser."

"Give me ten minutes," she said.

"Make it five. I'll text you when I'm out front of the Manor." He heard a sigh.

"Fine."

Then she hung up and Nate held on to his phone a second longer, tempted to call her back to suggest some alternative plan, but this was his chance to get to know more about her. It would also be an opportunity to establish boundaries if they were going to work together after all. That thought immediately raised an ironic smile as he pictured the kiss that almost happened yesterday. The one he was determined would not happen again.

He'd just pulled up in front of the Manor and was about to text her, when he saw her rental car rolling to a stop at the end of the driveway after all. He flashed his headlights, and she turned onto Church Street, heading to the junction at Route 7. He gave her a few minutes, thinking to put some space between them so once they got onto the highway other vehicles could separate them and not tie up traffic on the busy Route 7. It was a plan for only a few seconds because he realized he hadn't asked her which car rental they were aiming for. He heaved a sigh.

For some reason his cognitive abilities seemed to run at a slow speed whenever he was around

Annika Morrison. He tamped down on the accelerator and followed her out of Maple Glen.

She heeded every rule of the road, traveling almost five miles below the limit which he found slightly irritating and he wondered if she was making a point. Once she reached Bennington she slowed down even more, which Nate appreciated because following another vehicle in an urban setting wasn't easy. Plus, it was Saturday, and Nate noticed that everyone was taking advantage of the weather—sunny and warm for autumn—and the weekend. He peered up through the windshield, taking in the red, yellow and some orange leaves of the trees along the highway. Fall colors, and a big draw in Vermont for tourists. The locals were getting into the whole vibe, too, he thought. The streetlights in Bennington were wrapped with orange streamers for Halloween and perhaps even Thanksgiving, though by that time there could be snow on the ground.

Winter. Nate sighed again. He figured that there would be even less for him to do in Maple Glen. Fewer tourists accessing the Long Trail meant fewer illegally parked cars. Unless some resident went on a crime spree, life would definitely wind down. Time would stretch and he wasn't sure how he'd fill it. On the other hand, perhaps some downtime would be good for him, after the stresses of big-city living and policing in Boston.

He had a year to convince the residents and Bennington County Police that they needed a permanent sheriff for Otter Valley, including Maple Glen. There was a good chance he'd be leaving, and he felt an unexpected pang of regret. The idea of returning to Boston and a basically anonymous life there wasn't appealing, and Nate wondered how he'd weigh city versus country if he had to choose between the two jobs. He hoped his tenure in Maple Glen worked out, because he knew deep inside that there was no way he wanted to go back to that other life. He was still contemplating this future decision when he noticed Annika's signal light flashing and saw ahead a large sign for a car rental agency.

She was walking into the rental office as he was backing into a tight spot nearby. By the time he'd shifted into Park, she was opening the passenger door.

"Okay, well that's done," she said as she settled in and buckled her seat belt. "Thanks again, Nate. Now the cruiser?"

"The station isn't far...just on the outskirts of Wallingford where Route 7 merges into Church Street. Once we get there, you can simply go back to Maple Glen. You won't need to wait for me." He looked both ways as he turned onto Route 7 and headed toward the station.

"You're trusting me to drive your car without following behind?"

"I think we've moved on from the whole driving thing, haven't we?"

"Heavens, I hope so!"

He had to laugh. "So, to change the rather tiresome subject of driving, what are your thoughts about Devon's request for help at the Halloween celebration?" When she didn't reply right away, he looked over and saw her staring thoughtfully out the windshield. "Trying to come up with an excuse to get out of it?"

Her sigh was the immediate answer. Then she said, "I have a feeling my half-sister is a force to be reckoned with. Small but mighty."

"Perhaps. I don't know her very well yet."

"Neither do I! We've only known each other a few days."

"Oh?" That got his attention. The car swerved slightly as he turned to look at her.

"It's a long story, but to sum it up, Devon and I only found out last Christmas that we shared the same father. Dad was a career military officer stationed in Germany where he met my mother. They had a whirlwind courtship and when he retired from the army they moved to New Hampshire. It wasn't until after he died when I was fifteen, that my mother learned he'd been previously married and divorced. It was a shock, as you can imagine. The biggest shock though, came when she learned that he'd left behind two other children—Chloe and Billy Morrison, who later changed their names to Devon and Dan Fairchild."

She paused for a long moment. Calming herself, he wondered?

"I don't think my father knew his first wife—Devon's mother—had passed away until much later. I do know that his attempt to reunite with his children was foiled by some bureaucratic error, and then he had a heart attack before he could continue his search for them."

Nate took a minute to ponder that. He hadn't known that Devon was once Chloe Morrison. Walter Ingram's role in the discovery of the missing children on the Appalachian Trail had been extensively covered, but the names of the children had been redacted because they were in the foster care system. Learning that she had a half-sister must have raised lots of conflicting emotions for Annika, and he could relate.

Until his mother's death almost a year ago, he'd had no information at all about his biological father. After he found her letter, he'd searched online for references to Walter Ingram and learned that the man lived near Maple Glen. They had yet to meet but soon would. Privately.

"You both have had a lot to process," he said, "not only the details of your father's past, but these new complexities in both your lives. You're siblings who've only discovered each other. Maybe the best course is to take your time. Get to know her before the story becomes public knowledge in Maple Glen." When she didn't speak, he saw her nodding, assessing his advice.

Finally, she turned his way and smiled. "Good idea, Sheriff Gallagher."

He kept his eyes on hers as long as he safely could, then focused back to the road ahead. After a few minutes he said, "Tell me about your podcasting. How did you get into that?"

"I majored in journalism in college and planned to apply to various media companies after graduation, but my best friend and I heard a podcast series about someone who was convicted of a crime and spent years proving his innocence. We were mesmerized. Everything about the series was compelling—the facts of the case as well as the narrator's voice. Liz and I came up with an idea to do a podcast about current campus issues that affected students, instructors and administration. We did our best to balance all the sides."

"I suppose that was the trickiest part, wasn't

it? The balancing? Surely at some point you must have had to state your personal views."

He thought back to his time in Boston, his determination to expose the corruption he saw in his precinct, and his ultimate failure to change the system.

"Yes, but we kept that part for the summation."

"Then what? After college, I mean?"

"Have you ever heard of a company called Venture Media? It's headquartered in New Hampshire, where I hale from."

"No, but I grew up in Boston."

"Well, it's one of the biggest media corporations in the state and someone in their marketing department heard one of our podcasts and liked it and…the rest is history."

"History? How?"

"We developed a series called *We Reveal It*, focusing on local politics in New Hampshire. One of our episodes centered on a wealthy businessman in Concord who donated a lot of money to a local candidate running for mayor."

"So? I'm sure that happens everywhere and all the time."

"Yes, but not long after the candidate won the election, the businessman was given the okay to develop a large tract of land that had been designated 'green' by the previous council.

Fortunately, someone in administration found a loophole that got the council out of the original deal and the mayor was pressured to resign."

When she paused, Nate figured she was mentally reliving the whole unhappy business.

"You know that expression 'shoot the messenger'? Despite a good outcome for the citizens of Concord, my partner and I took the brunt of the outrage. Venture Media opted not to renew our contract to avoid any possible litigation."

"Sadly, those kinds of shady deals happen everywhere. Who knows, maybe something like that has happened even here."

"In Maple Glen?"

He heard the mock horror in her voice and laughed. "I guess anything can happen anywhere there are people with stories."

"And secrets most of all."

"Are local secrets the theme of your new podcast series then?"

"Oh no. As I told you, I'm going to be writing about local legends and folklore. That's the topic of my new pitch to Venture Media. There's a lot riding on getting a new contract. Not only my personal finances—" she uttered a sigh "—but my credibility as a podcast journalist. Plus, I doubt Venture will give me another chance. This is it. So, if any local secrets emerge from my research, well…"

Nate was saved from commenting when he spotted the police station ahead, and a cruiser parked in front of it. As he handed Annika his car keys, he quelled the urge to remind her to follow the speed limit. Instead, he said, "Just leave the car on the street outside my house. It's the one between Will Bower's house and his big maple syrup shed. And…uh…thanks for taking the time to do this, Annika."

"At the moment, time is what I have plenty of, Nate."

He ignored her slightly flirtatious tone, hearing instead the silent message beneath it. Loneliness maybe, or a sense of disconnect with others? Perhaps another similarity between them, he thought. "I suppose you'll be busy soon enough, working on your new podcast idea."

"And working with you, too, on the Halloween committee."

He saw the mischievous spark in her blue eyes and felt the irresistible lure of her grin. "I look forward to it," he said, keeping his tone as neutral as possible.

"Likewise, Sheriff Gallagher," she quipped.

Later that night Nate searched the Venture Media website for one of her podcasts but could find only one from almost a year ago. The series was called *We Reveal It* and the particular episode revealed corruption in the building industry in a small town in New Hampshire.

Nate had only listened to a few podcasts in his life and was no judge of the medium but found Annika's style edgy and assertive. He figured the targets of her exposé hadn't been happy with her afterward, which might explain why she'd opted to pitch a different idea to the company.

Nate knew nothing he'd learned was reason for suspicion about Annika Morrison's past or her purpose in Maple Glen and he figured the determination he'd seen in her eyes and heard in her voice earlier that day could guarantee success with her new idea. What worried him was her reference to uncovering local secrets. Still, working with her would allow him to pre-empt any revelations that might lead to problems with the local residents for her as well as for him.

ANNIKA WISHED SHE could hit Replay and delete all the silly comments she'd made to Nate on the way to the Bennington police station. He'd shown a sincere interest in her work, and she'd been almost flirtatious, a realization now that made her cringe.

For some reason the man brought out the worst in her. Right from the moment he caught her using his telescope to spy on the Manor, to her acting as if they'd never met at Devon's dinner party. She had no excuse for her behavior, and to his credit, he hadn't even mentioned that first encounter with her. Now that they'd be working together on a committee for the village Halloween celebrations, she'd need to get serious and stop behaving like a smitten teenager.

She didn't learn about Nate's formal introduction to the people of Maple Glen at the community center until Sunday morning, when Devon texted to ask if she intended to go to the event.

Annika texted back. What event?

Sheriff Gallagher's formal introduction to the community. A meet-and-greet, at four o'clock. Walk over with us and come back here for dinner. We've invited Nate, too.

Dinner sounded great, considering she had more ice cream on hand than anything nutritious, and another get-together with Nate was inevitable, given the size of Maple Glen. Yet she'd have liked a gap of at least forty-eight hours to allow her a chance to make some notes on how a possible collaboration with him might work. *Assuming it still happens*, she thought. Then she smiled. *Of course it's going to happen, silly. Otherwise, what excuse will you have to ensure more contact with the gentle sheriff?*

And he seemed gentle. Deep inside, and in

a complex way. Fair, too, though not a chump. She thought with some embarrassment about her light flirtation when he pulled her over for speeding. A deadpan face had been his response, along with a curt warning. Tall enough, and definitely handsome, though not in a classical way. A man like Sheriff Nate most certainly would have had someone special in his life. Maybe still did. She felt a stab of jealousy for that unknown woman, then reminded herself she had a mission in Maple Glen, and it wasn't to fall for a man whose job might become a lot more serious and complicated due to her podcast work.

Because overnight she'd had another idea for a podcast episode, connected to local people in Maple Glen and what secrets they held. She sensed that Nate might have a secret or two, and she figured some online research would eventually reveal them. Of course, all that raised the question—was she willing to expose them at the risk of jeopardizing a chance with Sheriff Gallagher?

CHAPTER SIX

NATE GRIPPED THE sides of the podium and took three calming breaths as he gazed out at the crowd of people sitting, some a bit restlessly, in the community center gym. Finn had just introduced him as the new interim sheriff of Otter Valley and was descending the portable steps pushed against the stage. After his brief intro, Finn had given Nate a quick pat on his shoulder as he lowered the microphone to Nate's height. He had meant the pat to be reassuring, Nate knew, but instead it had only raised his stress level. Though not as much as sighting Annika Morrison, with a notebook on her lap, perched on a chair in the middle of the first row of seats before him.

It was a bright fall day and even at four o'clock, the sun streamed through the windows on both sides of the gym. Like a spotlight, Nate thought. Finn had reminded him that because he was sheriff of the whole valley, people from Wallingford and smaller communities outside

Maple Glen would be interested in meeting him and hearing his plans for policing the area. As he waited while latecomers searched for empty chairs, he wondered if Walter Ingram was in attendance. There were many gray- and white-haired residents in the audience.

"Thanks, Chief McAllister," he began, "for organizing this opportunity to meet the citizens of Otter Valley." A breath and a pause, then he spotted someone taking a seat at the back of the gym. A tall gray-haired man with a cane. *Walter Ingram?*

He took a longer, deeper breath. "As some of you may already know, my tenure as sheriff here is temporary—an interim one—and a decision regarding its permanency will be made by the valley residents, as well as by the Bennington County Council, one year from now. The position is a Monday to Friday, nine to five job for the moment and calls or emergencies outside those times will be automatically redirected to the Bennington County Police Department."

A hand shot up. Annika Morrison. He opted to ignore her, not wanting to lose the momentum of his address. "I've already been informed by Sheriff Anderson, that there's one current issue troubling people here in Maple Glen itself." He noted Annika lowering her hand and people suddenly stopped fidgeting. This was definitely an issue, he thought, wishing he'd paid more attention to it when he was jotting the outline for his talk.

"Parking on Church Street." He paused until everyone was listening. "I have some ideas to address the problem, especially in high tourist season as visitors come to see the fall colors as well as accessing the shortcut to the Long Trail. It's a complex issue, because many businesses in Maple Glen and the valley in general look forward to the income generated by tourism, especially prior to winter when fewer people come to these parts. At the same time, people who live along Church Street may need or want access to parking as well."

Hands shot up, including Annika's again. Nate took a chance and called on her to speak. "Yes, um…in the front row."

When she stood, he heard a low buzz of whispers. People trying to identify her, he supposed. As the gym quietened down, she asked, "What are those ideas, Sheriff Gallagher?"

"Ticketing will be a start," he said. The buzz in the room amplified.

"That will work for out-of-state license plates," Annika said, "but what about the Vermont plates? How will you ascertain which cars are local or not?"

Someone called out, "Right on!"

Short of logging into a computer system for vehicle registration every time, there was only one way. Parking permits. Nate guessed that would provoke even more ire from the locals, although it was basically the best solution. It was also one that depended on support and approval from the Bennington County Police Department as well as the county council, but he had a feeling many Glen residents would be reluctant to change longtime habits. Still, he couldn't avoid the topic any longer. He took a deep breath and said, "Parking permits."

The uproar was deafening, though judging by some nods not everyone was opposed to the idea. When voices subsided, Nate continued. "The permits will allow for an equitable use of Church Street, and they don't have to be expensive. The amount can be decided by the council. Permits should also be granted to tourists who want to access the Long Trail from here. Those temporary permits can be any price the council chooses. Perhaps enough to boost the budget here for snow removal, waste collection and whatever services residents need and want." When Annika's hand rose again, he signaled her to speak.

"And the penalty for parking without a permit?"

"A ticket."

"And what department will ensure that people, especially tourists from out of state, will pay those tickets?" she asked.

Nate hadn't yet figured out all the details. "The Bennington County Council will have to collaborate with its police department on that because my jurisdiction is, for now, limited to Otter Valley." That seemed to satisfy many in the audience and when there were no more questions, Finn stood up from his seat in the front row.

"Thank you, Sheriff Gallagher. And a reminder to folks here that elections for positions on the Bennington County Council will also be held in a year, around the same time that Sheriff Gallagher's position comes up for review. So, if you have issues and concerns to address, running for election to the council is one way to help solve the problem."

There was a light titter of laughter before he added, "I've been asked to tell you that tea, coffee and cookies will be served in the smaller Youth Club room across the hall."

People began to get up, chatting to one another as they walked out of the gym and across the hall. Nate waited at the front of the room, hoping he could slip away and avoid the refreshment area where he imagined he'd be cornered by residents eager to continue the discussion or to air a grievance. He especially didn't want the occasion to be the place where he came face-to-face with Walter Ingram. That meeting was going to be private.

Finn must have noticed his hesitation because he came up to him and said in a low voice, "When you get into the hall, there's a door leading directly to the kitchen—and it's marked 'Kitchen'—where you'll find a delivery exit to the parking lot."

"Thanks for the tip. I'm not great at socializing in a crowd."

"You gave them the information they needed and that's enough. Socializing is a small part of the job, but I suspect you've already figured out how to appropriately balance that."

"This parking permit issue..."

"Change will always be a challenge for some people, but as they say...the greater good. Right?" Finn grinned.

"And balance, too. I assume as a member of the Bennington County Council, you'll be raising the permit and ticketing issue at the next meeting?"

"Tomorrow morning at nine thirty and I'm inviting you. Permits will be number one on the agenda along with parking tickets." He raised his broad shoulders in a "who knows?" gesture, smiled and headed into the hall and the refreshment area.

Nate waited a few seconds longer before leaving the gym, then walked toward the kitchen door and the exit to the parking lot. When he turned around after ensuring the door closed behind him, he saw Annika leaning against one of the cars. His car.

"Sneaking off?"

He shrugged at her broad grin. "Caught me."

"Not that I blame you, Sheriff Gallagher."

"Nate. Let's drop the sheriff bit." It came out a tad edgier than he'd intended, but he was ready to put the whole coy act to rest.

"Yeah, sorry about that. I tend to overdo things."

"I've noticed."

She took her time responding. "I'm hoping you'll still work with me on an episode for my podcast. In some way. Even if only to give me comments and suggestions."

Nate untangled the rush of words, deducing what his help meant to her. Still, he took his time with a reply. His mind told him this wasn't a good idea, especially should any work and personal conflicts arise, but his heart was urging otherwise. The chance to spend more time with an intelligent and beautiful woman. What could go wrong?

"Where and when?" he finally asked.

"Um, my place?"

He thought about passing by the Manor again, on his way to her cottage which would provide more fodder for the gossip mill. His place was almost as visible, on the main street and at the junction where anyone coming and going from Maple Glen had to pass. Then he realized the most obvious place would be right there at the community center, where few people would wonder about a resident meeting with the new sheriff right after his introductory talk.

"Let's go back inside to the gym. Everyone's having refreshments across the hall and no one's going to think twice about seeing us chatting there."

"Sure," she mumbled.

He thought she seemed disappointed but didn't relent. Public places were always a better choice for awkward conversations and any discussion with Annika Morrison seemed, as far as he was concerned, potentially highly awkward. "Follow me." He led the way across the parking lot to the center's front door, ignoring her loud sigh.

A few people were already leaving the coffee room and nodded at Nate as he led Annika to the gym. Fortunately, it was empty, and he pulled together two chairs, gesturing for her to sit. Once seated, she took a notebook and pen from her handbag while he pulled his chair a bit closer to hers.

"First question," he began, immediately taking charge of the interview.

She gave a tight smile. "As you know, the topic for my series is folklore and legends connected to small towns and villages here in Vermont. At least one, maybe two, episodes will focus on stories or legends related to Otter Valley and in particular, Maple Glen."

"Right, but as a newcomer to the area I have no knowledge of local stories and therefore, can't see how I can possibly be of any use to you. Perhaps enlisting a longtime local resident is your best bet."

"Yes, and I'll be interviewing several people who've lived here for some time."

"Okay, sounds like a good start. How can I assist with that?"

"Not with the actual interviews, but with any issues or complaints that residents might bring to you, as the valley law enforcement."

"Right, so I have to interject here to say that issues or complaints are confidential. Unless you come to me with questions about an incident that you have personally experienced, there's very little I'd be able to discuss with you."

"Even if it's something that affects the public? Like the parking debate?"

He wasn't about to be dragged into a debate of

any kind with her. "There's the council meeting tomorrow about that issue and others."

She took her time accepting the fact that he wasn't going to cooperate further. Tucking her notebook and pen back into her handbag was the signal that he'd won the first round and Nate was relieved.

"All right, Sheriff Gallagher… Nate," she added a second later. "I suppose I'll have to go ahead with my podcast without your help unless—"

"Unless I change my mind," he preempted.

She gave a curt nod and stood up. "I guess that's it for now, then." Slinging her handbag over her shoulder, she added, "See you at dinner tonight. At the Manor. Seven o'clock."

Nate let out a long breath as she walked toward the central gym door, but he figured his reprieve was temporary. There was still dinner.

THE DINNER WASN'T the ordeal Annika had feared. Finn's mother, Marion, had arrived that morning to discuss some family business with her son and Devon, and was staying with them. Annika had liked her from the start.

"Meeting you," she'd told Annika on being introduced, "is a wonderful ending to the storybook mystery and romance of Devon and my son."

"An ending to one story and the beginning of another," Annika had said.

"Well put, my dear. I hear you're a writer and working on a podcast series. I have to admit I've never actually listened to podcasts, though think I certainly must, now that someone in the family produces them. Is that the right word… *produces*?"

"More or less. Teamwork is usually involved, though in my case, I'm on my own."

"Is that a good thing or…?"

Annika thought of Liz and how well they'd worked together. "I hope a solo effort will be good. Success depends on which media company airs them and how extensively."

"And what will be the theme of your podcasts? I mean, do you have a specific topic or do the topics vary from one episode to the next?"

"My topic for the trial episode—the one I pitched—was American folklore and I used the legend of Lake Champlain with its Champy character. For other episodes, I plan to write stories specifically relevant to small towns and villages—like Maple Glen, for instance." She saw Marion's eyes widen with interest and warmed to her even more.

"Then you will definitely want to speak to some of the elders in the village." She gave a quick laugh. "Excluding me, I should add, because I've always been one to keep to myself a bit. I mean, I participate and help to organize some village events and celebrations, like the Christmas Bazaar, but generally I'm not one to get on the phone and talk about things…or other people here. I've found there's nothing to be gained from gossip."

Unless it can help you sell a podcast, Annika was thinking. "By gossip, you mean the Glen grapevine?" she asked.

"Precisely." Marion shifted her gaze to the other side of the dining room where Devon and Finn, their arms wrapped around one another, were saying goodbye to a couple standing at the front door. Marion was clearly referring to the buzz in Maple Glen following Devon's rescue on the Appalachian Trail by her son, Finn, almost a year ago.

"Well, as they say, the truth will out," Annika said.

"Gossip isn't about truth," Marion countered, her voice rising. "People can be hurt by it."

"Yes," Annika murmured, wondering how she'd got herself into what her mother would call "a pickle." "But I put a lot of research into my podcasts, rather than only relying on local gossip."

"Good for you. Then I look forward to your first episode. Feel free to email me any questions about the valley and the Glen. Finn will give you my address. And now my age is telling me it's bedtime."

Annika smiled and felt herself relax as she watched Finn's mother head upstairs. She was beginning to think researching material for an episode set in Maple Glen might be more difficult than she'd anticipated. But she'd always liked a good challenge.

She walked to the hall closet where Devon had hung her coat a couple of hours ago and was slipping into it when Nate came up to her and asked, "Leaving now?"

"Yes."

"I'll walk with you," he said.

"I'm fine. I just live a few yards behind this house."

"I know you do. But it's a clear night. We might see some stars."

"An irresistible lure."

"I think so."

He clasped her by an elbow and guided her to the door where Finn was waving goodbye to another couple.

"You two off, now?" Finn asked, smiling.

"Yes, and please thank Devon for me," Nate replied. "I'll see you at the meeting tomorrow."

"For sure." Finn looked from Nate to Annika. "Don't keep this guy up too late."

Annika knew he was joking but was relieved there was no one else but the three of them to hear. She smiled and quickly stepped out onto the front verandah. She heard Nate behind her, saying something else to Finn, and then he was suddenly at her side. They walked together in silence until they reached the front gate of the Manor and Nate abruptly stopped.

"Look up there." He pointed upward. "Not a cloud in sight. We just might get lucky and see some shooting stars if we stand still and keep our eyes on the night sky."

Head raised, his face shone under a bright moon. He was…indescribable, Annika thought. Handsome, but beautiful—inside, too, the way he thought of others. A keeper for any smart and lucky woman. Annika edged closer to him, wishing she were that woman, but she knew in her heart that she wasn't. Her time in Maple Glen was temporary, limited to writing and submitting her new podcast. Once she'd reestablished her connection to Venture Media, ensuring more financial security, she'd be gone.

"There!" he suddenly exclaimed, turning to her.

The excitement in his voice shook her from the dismal thoughts of leaving Maple Glen—and Nate Gallagher.

"Did you see it? A shooting star, just over the woods."

She shook her head but was entranced by the glow in his face. When was the last time she herself had felt such enthusiasm or passion? She looked up into the dark sky but all she saw were the usual clusters of stars that she'd seen other nights and in other places.

"Um, no I missed it. Too bad we don't have that telescope you got when you were twelve."

He shifted his attention from the sky to her and smiled. "You remember that? From our walk home after dinner at the Manor?"

The expression in his eyes touched her. He was clearly moved that she'd remembered the story about his birthday gift and she wanted to hug him. "I do," she said, "and sometime, on another night like this, I'd like to look up at those stars through a telescope." She took a breath for courage. "With you."

"I'd like that," he said.

"Take a break from…you know…the work thing."

"All work and no play…" he murmured, placing his hands on her shoulders.

"You could tell me more about the constellations and galaxies, like the one you mentioned that night."

"The Fireworks Galaxy." He drew her into his arms.

"And tell me again why it's called that. Fireworks."

"I promise I will."

She rested her head against the crisp coolness of his down jacket and thought she could hear his heart thumping, or perhaps that was her own, pounding in her ears.

When he pulled back, just enough to lower his mouth to hers, the night sky disappeared.

CHAPTER SEVEN

NATE WAS AWAKENED in the middle of his very realistic dream about stargazing with Annika and especially their parting kiss last night when his cell phone rang. It was the station dispatcher, Shelley Barnett, calling.

"Morning, Sheriff Gallagher. I came in early to do some prep for your meeting with the council, and the voicemail here was full. Complaints."

Already? His first full day on the job? "What kinds of complaints?"

"Mostly all about the same thing."

"Which is…?"

"All the cars parked on Church Street near the community center had their windshields soaped overnight."

"Soaped? As in—"

"Bars of soap were wet, I suppose, and used to scrawl all over the windows, even the door windows. Plus, flyers that are basically fake parking tickets were placed under all the wipers."

It took him a few seconds to mentally unravel

her details, but Nate quickly concluded the act was a direct result of yesterday's public meeting. "Parking tickets or flyers?"

"Printed from a home computer, I'm guessing."

"You've seen a copy?"

"Lots. Someone dropped off a bagful of them here at the station. They were waiting at the front door when I opened up."

He heard her chuckle before she added, "Whoever did them even typed in a fine of one hundred dollars—which was spelled incorrectly, by the way—for parking illegally on Church Street. And illegally was also spelled wrong. I'm thinking maybe a kid?"

Or simply a bad speller, Nate almost said, until he thought the spelling might have been deliberate to throw them off, make people think the act was simply teenage vandalism.

"Okay. I'm going to head there right away to take some photos."

"What about all these voice messages reporting the car soaping?"

"Yeah, um, I hate to say this but can you—"

"Call everyone back?"

"I'm sorry, Shelley, but otherwise all those people will keep phoning. Just let them know I'm aware of the situation and am investigating." He heard her sigh.

"Yeah, okay. Part of the job. Meanwhile, I should remind you of the meeting this morning."

"At nine thirty. Right. So, I need to look into this prank, or whatever it is, beforehand. Thanks, Shelley."

He rubbed his face after he hung up and decided there was time for a shower, but not breakfast. He'd had a restless night following the dinner at the Manor. He could have left early, citing his upcoming first day as interim sheriff, and now wished he had. Instead, he and Annika had ended up leaving together. Finn had cracked a silly joke, warning her not to keep him out late and they'd only walked a few feet when Nate had kissed her.

That impulsive move tormented him all night long, especially after his vow to keep things on a neutral, friendly basis. Had it been the dress she'd been wearing—a blend of blues and greens—the perfect foil to her red hair? Her lips, slightly parted in awe as she gazed up at the sky? Or the look of wonder in her beautiful face as she looked for the shooting star?

Nate decided that had been the moment. Yet what did it matter now? He'd broken his own promise to himself when he was hired for this job. He'd known that he'd have to distance himself from members of the community, and especially not get emotionally involved with the very people he would have to police. He thought back to his first encounter with Annika, speeding on Route 7. The flash of her brilliant smile. At the time, he'd suspected the smile had been meant to charm him to avoid getting a ticket. The ploy had worked, although he hadn't been officially sworn in then so he couldn't have issued a ticket anyway. But she hadn't known that.

You've no one to blame but yourself, Gallagher, for crossing the line between work and romance. He sighed, rubbing his face, thinking of the day ahead.

And a hectic one it was going to be. He'd planned to pick up his set of uniforms on his way to the council meeting and use the station's restroom to change. Of course, now the councilors would have something far more important on their minds than a uniform. As he quickly pulled on jeans and a sweatshirt, Nate didn't know whether to laugh or feel sorry for himself. Then he had to search for his camera, still tucked inside a backpack in a closet. The station would have its own, but he wanted to take photos before owners washed the windows.

His car was parked in the driveway, but it was simpler to jog out to the street toward the community center. The scene of the crime. The descriptor seemed ludicrous given the minor damage, but Nate knew from experience that a deliberate act, even meant as a joke, could stem from an unresolved grudge or an old resentment. Someone in Maple Glen—or maybe even beyond—had a message to deliver.

Nate thought back to yesterday's community meeting and the mood of those attending as they'd left. After the initial outburst at his parking permit suggestion, he'd sensed a general acceptance of his plans, and no one had hung behind to vent sour feelings. Of course, he hadn't been in the village long enough to learn a lot about its residents. Those whom he'd met had been friendly and welcoming. Good people, his mother would have said. Yet policing experience had taught him that even good people erred when life presented difficult challenges.

He was almost at the community center when he was confronted by a couple lugging a bucket of water. Despite the fact he wasn't in uniform, they recognized him immediately.

"Sheriff Gallagher! We attended some of the community meeting yesterday and heard your plans about the parking problem." The man gestured to the cars behind him with the hand holding a scrub brush. "What are you going to do about this?"

Nate held up his camera. "I'm taking photos for my own investigation, and if people want to make insurance claims, I can provide copies."

They seemed mollified by his response, but the woman went on to say, "We thought it might be kids. Teenagers maybe, getting ready for Halloween next week."

Halloween. Nate had pushed that annual celebration out of his mind shortly after he'd been appointed to a committee for it. With Annika Morrison. That thought immediately segued to another. Where was she right now?

"Is soaping car windows a common prank at Halloween here, then?" he asked them.

They shook their heads. "This is a first," the woman said. "A phenomenon for the mellow people of Maple Glen!" she exclaimed, with a slight laugh.

Nate hoped it was a one-time phenomenon, and not an annual tradition. "Are you folks from here, then?"

"No, from Montpelier," the man answered. "But we always come to this area to see the fall colors on the Trail and thought we'd spend the night and do some hiking today. That is, until we saw our car."

"Where did you stay last night?"

"At the B and B down the street. We could have parked in the lot there, but we'd left our car on the street while we checked out the bakery and strolled around the village. We couldn't be bothered moving it again. If only..." The man shook his head. "Mr. Watson gave us the bucket and scrub brush."

"He seemed almost amused," the woman put in, scowling.

Yeah, Nate thought, that would be Bernie. He didn't know the man well but guessed from his comments the day Nate checked in that he was annoyed at some of the tourists descending on the village.

He thanked the couple and started taking photos as he reached the first few cars. He started with the windshields, then the license plates. All out-of-state cars had been soaped. That made sense to Nate if someone resented tourists using too many parking spaces on the main thoroughfare of the village. Except why target some of the Vermont cars, too? Unless the vandal knew those cars didn't belong to any local residents. In that case, the person responsible could be someone living in, or near, Maple Glen.

He'd photographed almost all of the cars when his cell phone rang. Finn McAllister. "Hey, Finn, I'm on Church taking photos, so I may be a bit late for the meeting."

"Yeah, I heard about the cars. Someone called Bennington Police and a cruiser has been dispatched, even though this area is Otter Valley and your jurisdiction. Also, the meeting this morning has been rescheduled for tomorrow so people will have more information about what's happened today."

Nate closed his eyes, wishing himself back in bed and starting the day all over again. "Anyone on Church have security cameras outside their homes?" he asked.

He heard a snort. "Seriously? This is Maple Glen, buddy. Stuff like this just doesn't happen here."

And yet it had, Nate thought. He was on his way home to upload his photos when he met a familiar figure walking his way. Annika. Could his day get any worse, he wondered, as he saw her pulling her cell phone out of her jacket pocket.

"Nate," she said as he drew closer, "any idea who's behind this prank?"

"A bit more than a prank, considering people have had to clean their cars this morning and will now be wary about parking here."

"I guess that's the point, isn't it? Discouraging outsiders from using the street for parking?"

It made sense. "That'll be a possible explanation to raise at the meeting tomorrow."

"Tomorrow? I thought it was today."

"It's been rescheduled so I can get more information about all this." He waved an arm toward the parked cars.

“Where will you start?”

“I’m going to the station to run license plates right now.”

She pulled one of the fake parking tickets from her pocket. “I wonder if these were deliberately made to look like some kid printed them out. They clearly wouldn’t fool an adult.”

“I don’t think they were meant to. Someone wanted to stir things up. Maybe someone who doesn’t like change here.”

She sniffed. “That could apply to almost everyone in Maple Glen, I think.”

“Is that your confirmation bias about small towns showing, Ms. Morrison?” He couldn’t resist the tease.

“Maybe,” she said, shrugging. “But it’s a bit of a coincidence, isn’t it? Perhaps the meeting gave that person an idea overnight.”

That’s what worried Nate. One bad idea sometimes led to others. “I’m cautioning you not to heighten community feelings by uploading those photos to your social media accounts,” he said.

“I will ascribe that comment to your stress at having to deal with this situation so early in the morning, Sheriff Gallagher.” She wheeled around and headed in the direction of the Manor.

He’d just proven his point about escalating bad ideas. Too bad he hadn’t followed his own advice.

WAS NATE GALLAGHER the problem, or was she? Annika stewed over that on her way back to her cottage. Their viewpoints were constantly flipping, from agreement to complete bewilderment with one another, and these reactions seemed to have worsened since the kiss. Or so it seemed to her, and she had a feeling he, too, felt the same. His comment about uploading photos of the vandalized cars had stung, especially since the thought *had* occurred—briefly—before she dismissed it.

She let out an exasperated breath as she turned into the Manor driveway. Coffee was what she needed and perhaps some distance from the sheriff to gain a better understanding of the man. She was passing the front door of the house when it swung open.

"Annika!" Devon called from the doorstep. "Come in for coffee and a chat."

She hesitated but knew she couldn't delay the conversation about their pasts with her half-sister. Nate would approve, she thought, recalling his advice the other day about meeting Devon away from the prying eyes of Maple Glen. She felt a twinge of guilt about avoiding a private meeting with Devon, especially since she'd been in Maple Glen since Wednesday, five days ago. She took a deep breath and crossed the lawn to the front door.

"Finn told me about the situation with the cars," Devon said as Annika mounted the verandah steps. "I guess people are upset?"

"More like puzzled," Annika said.

"So, not a Halloween prank? I mean, it's only a week or so away." She held open the door and gestured for Annika to go in.

"Nate thinks it's more than that. Something to do with the parking problem," Annika said as she walked into the entry hall. She paused for a minute, taking in the grand staircase ahead and the long corridor leading to the kitchen.

"Nate? Are you and the sheriff on a first-name basis then?"

Annika knew from Devon's grin that she was teasing. "Isn't everyone in Maple Glen on a first-name basis?"

Devon laughed at that. "True, and welcome to my world!"

"How do you stand it?" Annika asked as she slipped out of her jacket.

"I have strategies, believe me." She took Annika's jacket and hung it in a closet next to a small table featuring what looked like an antique lamp.

Nate would know for sure, Annika thought with a smile, remembering his fascination with the decor in the cottage. The sheriff again, popping into her thoughts at random, disorienting her. She pushed him from her mind as she followed Devon along the hall to the kitchen.

"I prefer this room to the fussiness of the front parlor," Devon said as she headed for a coffee machine on one counter.

Devon had told her she and Finn planned some major renovations after their wedding at Thanksgiving and that they'd be moving into the cottage when that happened. Almost a month away. Annika would have to move out, but that was okay with her. She'd intended to stay in Maple Glen only long enough for the wedding anyway. Small towns might be interesting as podcast subjects, but not as places for permanent living.

"What are your renovation plans?" Annika asked, sitting in one of the four chairs at the table.

"Just a superficial redo before the wedding. Some painting, moving some of the furniture into storage until Finn and I have a chance to talk about the house with his mother and sister. After that conversation, we'll make the actual renovation plans with an architect and construction company." She poured coffee into two mugs. "Milk? Sugar?"

"Just black, and…uh…why the house conversation then?"

She handed a mug of coffee to Annika before adding milk to her own. "Finn's mother has deeded the Manor to us as a wedding present, but we still feel obliged to consult her about renovations. She and Finn's father lived here for many years, and the house goes back at least two or three generations."

"I can't even think what that would be like… that kind of family history."

"Nor I," said Devon, sitting opposite her.

Annika blew gently on the hot coffee before sipping, waiting for her sister to break the long silence. When she didn't, Annika went ahead and asked, "What do you remember from your early childhood?"

Devon seemed to hesitate before answering. "Not much. Voices mostly, raised in anger. Then days when my mother slept a lot and Dan… I mean Billy…and I shuffled around the house. Sometimes foraging for our own food, looking after ourselves as best as a three-year-old and five-year-old could. Billy stopped going to school, so child services were contacted, and we were quickly placed in care because our father—Blake Morrison, whom we barely knew—was in the army, in Germany. I think our parents were already separated at the time, and our mother had severed all contact with him. Then, because of some bureaucratic oversight, no one connected us to him after she died. Our first foster home was with a couple who had two grown children of their own. They were nice. Warm and kind. But when the man developed some kind of health issue we were placed elsewhere."

Her long inhale of breath echoed in the quiet kitchen and Annika was beginning to regret her question, when Devon continued speaking.

"That placement wasn't good. Lots of arguing and…basically unhappiness, as I realize now. The couple—I've completely blocked their names—decided a holiday might improve things. As if!"

"And that's when you and your brother ran away." Annika almost said "our brother" but stopped herself. Billy, or Dan, was only a name to her, yet so much more to Devon, who grew up with him.

"Yes, and the rest is history, as the saying goes. We were very lucky that someone like Walter Ingram found us, because he sensed right away that we needed to be handed over to the Department for Children and Families rather than returned to those foster parents. Our next placement with Ellen and Ted was…well…life changing, literally. We were lucky, but we owed so much to Walter and to our new social worker, Amelia Owens. I just wish Dan could have lived long enough to meet Walter again, as I did." She managed a smile, but her hands trembled as she set down her coffee mug.

There were no appropriate words of comfort for what Devon surely must be feeling. Annika reached across the table and clasped her sister's hand in hers. When the silence continued long enough that Annika questioned whether she ought to leave, Devon suddenly asked, "What was our father like?"

The warmth of his memory was overwhelming, and Annika took a minute, allowing herself both the happiness and the sorrow it brought.

"You may have heard that he and my mother met when he was stationed in Stuttgart. She worked on the base there, and they fell in love. Mom didn't know he'd had children from a previous relationship until after he passed away. That's when your social worker found the letter he'd sent, asking for contact with you and your brother, and she subsequently gave that information to my mother and me." She paused, trying to wrangle all the disjointed memories and half memories together. "I don't know why Dad didn't pursue the matter further, especially when his tour of duty ended. Perhaps he'd always planned to, but then he had that fatal heart attack not long after he left the army so..."

Devon waited out the brief silence before adding, "I feel bad that I haven't even asked about your mother. She's still alive and—"

"Yes, living in New Hampshire. Concord. She

gave me her blessing to come here and, well, your wedding invitation provided the opportunity."

"I'm glad you came. I wasn't sure if you would, because we'd only emailed each other a few times and hadn't met in person." She withdrew her hand from Annika's as she leaned forward in her chair. "Tell me about our father—Blake Morrison. Would I have liked him?"

"Oh yes," Annika said, as she blinked away the dampness in her eyes.

Later, after Annika left Devon to process everything, she thought how circumstance or plain luck might guide a person through the maze of life, and the importance of choice in that journey. She hadn't always excelled at making good, personal choices, but perhaps she'd have the opportunity to change that pattern in Maple Glen with her new work project, and most of all, with a chance at the kind of love her parents—Blake and Anna—had found together.

CHAPTER EIGHT

NATE WAS STUMPED. After he'd seen off the officer from Bennington, apologizing for the mix-up in communications, he'd returned to the station to run the license plates of the soaped cars. Shelley presented him with the bag full of flyers. If he'd been in Boston, he might have been able to dust a few of the flyers for fingerprints, but there was no such kit available. Something else to add to the "wish" list he planned to present at the council meeting tomorrow morning.

One vehicle was from Montpelier and another from Burlington, while the rest were from Wallingford and Maple Glen itself. He'd phoned Bernie Watson and learned that the people from Montpelier—the pair he'd met washing their car windows earlier that morning—had checked out. The Burlington owners had stayed at the Shady Nook but were hiking the Trail, and not due to return until the next day, planning to camp overnight. Nate silently wished them luck, because the weather forecast wasn't great.

Shelley had made a list of those people who'd called to complain, and he was checking through it to connect their names to the plates when his cell phone rang. There was no caller ID, but Nate knew his contact list would expand quickly, especially after the overnight car soaping. He sighed when he heard Annika Morrison's voice.

"Hi, Nate. I had an idea after our chat earlier this morning about the parking problem. The prank or whatever it was and…uh…thought since there are no security cameras on the street that maybe someone could…you know…do some surveillance. Overnight."

And one he'd already considered. "Um, yes that's a possibility."

Silence on the other end of the line. Nate wondered if she was thinking back to yesterday after the community center meeting when she'd suggested they could work together on village issues by sharing information about people in Maple Glen, and he'd squelched that idea right away.

"I'm sure you've already thought of that though," she quickly said. "The other reason I'm calling is that I plan to arrange an interview with Walter Ingram for my podcast episode."

Nate tightened his grip on his phone. "Okay."

"Have you met him yet? I just wonder how I should approach him. I mean, there's sort of a family connection with Devon, but I have a feeling he might be wary of any more publicity… considering."

No kidding, Nate was thinking. "Maybe talk to Devon about that."

"Um, sure. I thought you might be interested in coming with me."

"Why is that?"

There was a long pause and Nate figured she'd heard his reluctance loud and clear.

"No special reason, just for moral support I guess, and thinking you'd probably be connecting with him eventually anyway."

"*Eventually* is the key word. Now, is there anything else? I've work to do."

"Of course. Sorry to interrupt. I'll let you get back to…um…your busy day."

Message received and processed, Nate decided. When she hung up, he felt a small twinge of guilt, but she needed to know they might share information occasionally, but they definitely weren't working together. He was regretting his decision to encourage a friendship with Annika Morrison.

Friendship! Who are you kidding, Gallagher? The kiss on the way home from dinner at the Manor wasn't the kind friends exchanged, and was his first, and biggest, mistake since taking the job as sheriff. One he wouldn't repeat, and he had to reset the boundaries, even if it meant making Annika think less of him. He ought to have clarified his feelings and intentions right away and would have if they hadn't gazed upward at stars and constellations. The perfect conclusion to a magical moment.

He stared blankly through the glass window of his office, watching Shelley on the station landline in the other room. The desktop computer on her desk was from another era, too, and Nate wondered if he should add office upgrades to his wish list at the council meeting. Perhaps not, he decided, thinking requests of elected officials were sometimes best handled step by step.

The parking permit issue was the priority because it clearly affected the whole community and how he managed it would determine the length of his tenure as sheriff. He wanted any decision about leaving Maple Glen when his year was up to be his, and not Bennington County's.

The day ahead was promising to be a long one and Nate, used to more active policing in Boston, was itching to move. Was it too early for a coffee break, he wondered? He stared at the machine Shelley had brought from home and set up before he'd come on duty that morning. The extra caffeine might worsen his restlessness, though. He sighed and returned to the list of names and license plates. Minutes later, when he noticed

Shelley beckoning him, he was grateful for the chance to get up and stretch.

"Your uniforms are ready to be picked up in Bennington," she said as he reached his office door. "Want me to go get them?"

She seemed as eager as he was to get out of the office, but he had a better excuse. "Thanks, but I should go. I'll probably need to try one on, make sure they fit." He felt bad at the disappointment in her face. "Look, if you can just finish those phone calls that would be great. Take a break for a bit, have an early lunch, and I'll get back as soon as I can." The last sentence did the trick, as her expression perked up.

"I'm almost done here anyway. All the cars, except for the couple from Montpelier and that one where the people are hiking on the Trail, belong to Maple Glen folks, except for one registered to someone living in Wallingford. I've got her name and address here." She waved a Post-it at him.

"That's great, Shelley, I'll contact her, and thanks again for coming in early today."

"Did Sheriff Anderson tell you my workday is eight to four? Cause I need to be home for the school bus."

"Right, he did. That's okay by me and let me know if you need extra time at either end of the day. I know you have young children."

"Not that young. They're a preteen and teenager, but I don't want them to be on their own for too long. If we lived closer to Maple Glen, they'd have access to the Youth Club and some of the programs at the community center."

"Nothing like that in Wallingford?"

"Sure, but they're costly, and I'm a single parent so…"

Nate thought about his childhood and preteens when he'd spent many long, and sometimes unhappy, hours at various daycare or after-school programs in Boston. "Never hesitate to ask for the time, Shelley."

She managed a smile, but he thought she might be close to tears. "Uh, I should go," he said. "If I'm not back when you have to get home, just lock up. I've a feeling police work here might be—"

"A bit slow?" She was smiling now. "Sheriff Anderson probably told you most of the job is managing complaints—a lot of them petty ones."

"Yeah, he did. Though maybe this parking permit thing might lead to something bigger."

She nodded and pointed to the bag of fake tickets on the floor near her desk. "I think it already has, Sheriff Gallagher."

ANNIKA KNEW A brush-off when she got one. There'd been many in her life, and not all of them connected to her work in journalism. She couldn't really blame Nate, because she'd been a tad persistent that morning. Make that annoying, Morrison. All part of a journalist's job, and she figured he would know that.

The role of sheriff in Otter Valley wasn't his first gig in policing, as her internet search had revealed, though the reasons for his resignation from the Boston Police Department were vague. As in politically vague, but Annika knew how to read between the lines of official police press statements. He'd overreached the parameters of his rank, she guessed from the article, which hinted at a dispute between him and senior officials, and one that he clearly didn't back down from. Annika felt that persistence was a trait they shared, and despite his not-so-subtle message that they couldn't work together, she wasn't ready to give up.

After the awkward phone call, she needed physical exercise to clear her head and decided to visit the farm shop, conveniently located behind Nate's house. Her visit to the shop would serve a dual purpose, for she might find some of Walter Ingram's honey and bee products, or even the man himself.

She wished she'd spoken to Devon about arranging a meeting with him because she still hoped to interview him for one of her episodes.

Not to reveal Devon's story or their family connection, because she'd never exploit her half-sister's experience, but to highlight a local hero. The series would benefit from a human-interest story, especially as an introduction to local legends. After all, didn't most legendary characters spring from larger-than-life real people?

The day was typical for autumn, with a suggestion of winter added to the last rays of summer's warmth. A fleecy cardigan was all Annika needed over her T-shirt and jeans, and as soon as she stepped outside, she felt a surge of adrenaline from the hope of an interview. She'd considered bringing her notebook but guessed Walter would be leery of anyone resembling a journalist or reporter. Perhaps she could use her friendship with the new sheriff as an introduction. Name-dropping had become one of her talents while she was writing her *We Reveal It* podcasts for Venture Media and though Maple Glen was worlds away from that life, Annika knew names still mattered in the village.

She stepped onto Church Street and headed for the farm shop, directly behind Nate's house. His car was gone, of course, because he was at the police station, sorting out the mess from the morning's soaped windows fiasco. She was still irked by his caution about uploading photographs of the scene, even if his assumption had been close to the mark. What bothered her more was the thought that his opinion of her might change if she'd done so. Despite the dangers inherent in a "more than friends" relationship with the handsome sheriff, a part of Annika wanted to hold on to that possibility as long as she could, though she was beginning to realize the odds were against her now.

There were only a couple of vehicles in the small parking lot next to the farm shop, but it was late afternoon on a Monday and Annika figured peak times were weekends and holidays. She pushed open the main front door, fashioned out of what looked like an old piece of barn wood. The bright vaulted ceiling with skylights cast shafts of autumn gold onto the displays and Annika thought the place would glow even on cloudy days, with the floor-to-ceiling windows along both sides of the building.

At the far end of the shop, she spotted two women chatting and as she drew closer recognized one of them as the owner—Leni Bower—the woman who'd been sitting next to Nate at Devon's dinner party. Not wanting to intrude on their conversation, Annika simply gave a small wave and began browsing. The selection was overwhelming, and she was quickly swept up in the variety of jars of preserves, bottles of vinegars and olive oils, baked goods from what looked like artisanal shops from elsewhere though she spotted some with Tasty Delights labels, the Maple Glen bakery. There were large, refrigerated cases of meats and dairy products as well as bushel baskets of fresh produce and flowers.

Eventually she found what she'd been looking for. Two tables devoted to products from bees and honey. One featured items made from beeswax—candles mainly—but also creams for face and hands. She picked up a small jar labeled Bee Balm and glancing at the underside, saw that it had been made by Leni herself, with an added message: From Walter Ingram's Apiary. She took the jar and walked toward the rustic counter in the center of the shop. As she reached it, Leni was heading her way, smiling.

"Hello! We met at Devon and Finn's place, didn't we? You're—"

"Annika. Devon' s sister," she said. "This is a lovely shop, Leni."

"Thank you. The culmination of an old dream of mine, with lots of help from good friends, my family and an amazing husband."

Her happiness touched Annika, in spite of her own tendency to be a bit cynical about romance and love. "I'll take this for now," she said, handing Leni the jar, "but plan to come back for some gift shopping later." As Leni wrapped the jar in tissue paper, Annika asked, "Does Walter come into the shop often?"

Leni shook her head as she passed her the bag. "No, unfortunately. He has hip problems and doesn't get out as much as he used to. I'm sure at some point you'll meet him, though, because he's a bit more sociable these days than he used to be, despite his mobility issues."

"Oh?"

"Thanks to Amelia Owens." She must have registered Annika's puzzled expression. "Um, you should ask Devon about Amelia."

Leni was a loyal friend who'd clearly decided she'd passed on enough information. "I will, because I'm interested in meeting him. I don't know if Devon has told you, but I'm working on a podcast series about folklore and legends in small-town America. I think Walter would be the perfect subject for an episode."

"Hmm, well…perhaps."

The change in Leni's face and manner was like a door closing. More like slamming, Annika thought. "But of course, all that depends on his willingness to be interviewed."

"And good luck with that," was all Leni said.

Annika waited a beat for Leni to go on, then asked, "What do I owe you for the cream, Leni?"

Leni waved a hand. "On the house."

"No way, this is your business," Annika said.

"Nope. A gift to my best friend's sister."

Annika felt her face heat up. There was no good way to extricate herself from the awkward moment. "Well, thank you very much, Leni. And I'll definitely be back shopping for gifts before I leave Maple Glen."

"Have you set a date for that?"

Annika was unsure if Leni was merely curious or hinting at a possible departure. "Not really. I mean, my sister's wedding isn't until Thanksgiving. I haven't decided to stay till then or go back to New Hampshire and return later for the celebration."

"I'm sure Devon and the rest of the family will be thrilled to have you."

Annika hoped so, though she couldn't be quite so certain about the family's reaction if her plan to feature Walter Ingram in her episode about Maple Glen panned out. He was a very private person, and she guessed Devon and family—perhaps most of Maple Glen—respected that trait. But he was also a local hero, one she believed ought to be celebrated. Something she sincerely wanted to achieve through a podcast.

CHAPTER NINE

NATE JUMPED AT a sudden rap on his driver's side window. He must have drifted off, because he had to take a second to orient himself. In his car, at night, parked on Church Street. The windshield had steamed up, likely from his breathing, because he'd been slumped over the steering wheel. He pushed the window button and saw Annika holding up a thermos and grinning.

"Guess I'm getting this to you just in time." She handed him the thermos and walked around to the passenger side to climb inside.

"How did you know I was here?" he asked, as he unscrewed the thermos cap.

"I went for a walk after dinner and saw your car, with you in it. Is this what's called a stakeout? Cause you're not exactly hidden."

He enjoyed a long swig from the thermos. She did make good coffee. "I know. Someone walking by will easily spot me, but not someone driving. They'll be looking ahead and seeing only a line of parked cars." He gulped more coffee. "Thanks for this. I seriously needed caffeine."

"Do you think there's any point sitting here all night? I mean, is it likely whoever soaped the cars will come back and do it again?"

"Not that, but perhaps something else. I've a feeling someone wants to make a point and won't give up unless—"

"The council backs down on their decision to bring in parking permits?"

"It could, if enough people make a fuss about all this. Community voices matter to elected officials."

"Sure, but the election's a year away."

Nate sighed. "That's what's bugging me. Why bother then? Unless…"

"Someone wants people to stop coming to Maple Glen. But why?"

He'd given that question some thought before falling asleep. "Maybe to discourage them from accessing the Long Trail here."

"I'm still not getting your point."

"If tourists don't access the Trail here, where's the next entry?" he asked.

"Um, I'm kind of new to the area, remember? I've no idea."

"The main entry gate in this area is in Wallingford at White Rocks Recreation Area."

"And? Sorry, but I'm tired and think I might need a hit of that coffee, too."

He handed her the thermos. "If tourists can't park here, then they can't enter the Trail here. Then—"

"They'll have to use the gate in Wallingford."

"Keep going."

"So, someone in Wallingford wants people to use the entry there."

"And?" He was teasing her, but the talk was also keeping him awake.

"That will keep more tourists in Wallingford, instead of luring them to Maple Glen." She thought for a minute, then said, "It still doesn't make a lot of sense. People would have to know about the access to the Trail here, as I'm betting it's not mentioned on any official website."

"You're right, but it is highlighted on social media." He picked up his cell phone from the dashboard, scrolled through his bookmarks and then handed it to her.

"Sheesh. Who knew Maple Glen was a *thing*?"

"Well, not the village per se, as much as its accessibility to the Trail. Obviously, there's some payoff to businesses here, too. I mean, the bakery always seems to have long lineups, and those customers can't all be from Maple Glen."

"But what other nearby businesses are there?"

"The store attached to the gas station on Route 7?"

"Not serious competition, believe me. I've been in it." The day she first drove to Maple Glen, after being pulled over for speeding by the man next to her. The stale Twinkie and watery coffee hadn't impressed her.

He laughed at her expression but got her point. The main reason to use Maple Glen's access to the Trail was its convenience, plus the fact that parking was free. "After I picked up my uniforms, I drove to the Wallingford gate. The parking lot there is currently being outfitted with parking meters."

"Oooh, so hikers will be paying to park now, and if they're planning to camp and spend a couple of days in the park—"

"The fees will add up."

"But won't permit parking here discourage those people? They'd still have to pay to park."

"Permits, even temporary ones for hikers and campers, will be cheaper than parking meters, which will be based on hourly rates," Nate said.

"True. Then why the fuss from village residents about the permits? It seems to me that hikers are going to want easy access points to the Trail and unless that entry point here in the Glen is closed, they'll continue to park here. What does Finn have to say about all this? Doesn't he have something to do with the Trail?"

"He's a volunteer, but one of only a few in this part of the park. He'll be attending the meeting in Bennington to argue for permit parking, because serious and experienced hikers will pay for the permits, whereas—"

"Tourists who come for the scenery and so on, might impulsively decide to go for a hike, but won't have a permit and probably won't want to bother getting one. So, the whole permit thing will be a waste unless you hand out tickets. Which will annoy people who live here all the more."

Nate smiled. She was way ahead of him. Maybe he ought to consider deputizing her. "Well, definitely some of them will be annoyed but I think people who live in the Glen will comply with the permits once they're used to the change."

"Maybe, but after the public meeting last Sunday..."

"Yeah. Though perhaps now people will see things differently."

"Or be even more upset," she said.

That's what worried him. The last thing he needed was to have an escalation of bad feelings, which would inevitably lead to bad, as in illegal, actions. He felt the flyers didn't constitute an illegal act, so much as mischief. Which could lead to a charge, though he'd worry about the legalities when he had a suspect, which reminded him to contact the woman from Wallingford whose information Shelley had jotted on the Post-it note.

He let out a sour breath. Where was that note now? It was hard to think straight with Annika sitting next to him, close enough for him to catch a faint waft of a floral scent every time she moved. He felt around in the jeans jacket he was wearing, then tried his shirt pockets and let out another long exhale, this time one of relief as he pulled out the note.

"I think we can scrap the surveillance," he said. "Shelley gave me some info about one of the cars that I'll follow up in the morning. It may be a lead, or not." He waved the Post-it at her but it fell to the floor, and they both ducked for it.

She reached it first, holding it aloft with her thumb and middle finger. "Ta-da! What'll you give me for it, Sheriff Gallagher?"

His face was inches from hers, his senses overwhelmed with flowery fragrances, caffeine and fatigue. Nate placed a finger under her chin and gently brought her face even closer. Then he closed his eyes and let his lips answer for him.

ANNIKA WAS AWAKENED early the next morning by her cell phone lighting up with a text notification. She was groggy from lack of sleep and fumbled the phone when she reached for it on her bedside table, almost dropping it.

Halloween Committee meeting this morning at my place, 9:30. Coffee and refreshments will be served! Devon

Devon really is keen, Annika thought. Then she noticed Nate's name on the recipient list and groaned. There really was no escape from encountering people multiple times in Maple Glen. Still, maybe having other people around as buffers would be a good way to handle their first meeting after last night's awkward ending.

The kiss and what it might portend kept her awake off and on through the night. She bet he'd had a restless sleep, too, because she was certain he'd enjoyed the kiss as much as she had. That brief kiss might have led to a longer moment had it not been interrupted by a car's headlights streaming through his rear window.

Nate had placed his hand on the back of her head and hissed, "Stay down!" The only sounds in his car had been his breathing and the pulse of her heart pounding in her ears.

When the beam of light shone on the parked

cars ahead, Nate had wriggled over, slowly opened his door and slipped out onto the road, carefully closing the door behind him. Annika had risked a quick glance upward through the windshield, ducking back down again when she saw the car make a U-turn and head back toward them. She hadn't seen Nate but guessed he was crouching at the side of the road. When the car had passed by, Annika had popped up again to see Nate taking a photo of the license plate with his cell phone.

He'd waited on the road until the mystery car's taillights disappeared into the dark, then climbed back into his car. "Same license plate," he'd murmured, gazing down at the photo. Then he'd held up the Post-it, the one they'd reached for together. That had led to the kiss, and how the evening had almost ended.

She groaned again, texted a hasty *ok* to Devon and threw back the comforter that she'd been entangled in all night. Coffee and refreshments provided the motivation to propel her into the bathroom for a quick wash, then into jeans and sweater. Same jeans, different sweater than yesterday. She was beginning to realize another trip to the Bennington mall might be in the works and sighed.

Meeting her half-sister for the first time, checking out the village for possible podcast ideas. Venture Media had given her a chance at another pitch and the deadline was the first week in November, mere days after Halloween. She figured this was her last shot at working with the company and she had to succeed.

Then she'd go back to New Hampshire before her inevitable return at Thanksgiving for Devon's wedding. That was it.

Now everything was muddled, something even she, as a habitual non-planner, found challenging. And all due to a certain sheriff, she thought, as she got dressed and headed down the drive to the Manor.

"Family get to walk right in," Devon told her as she opened the front door.

"You forget I grew up in Concord, where doors are always locked."

"Glad I missed that part," Devon said.

Was time really a healer, Annika wondered? Devon seemed testament to that adage, though from their talk the other day, Annika knew life and its effects on a person weren't so easily categorized.

She pushed the thought aside as she followed her sister into the dining room and was introduced to four women already seated at the table. "Ladies, I'd like you to meet my sister, Annika Morrison."

The chatter came to an abrupt halt.

"You've already met Leni, at my place," Devon said, looking at Annika. "This is Maura, who owns Jake & Friends riding stables, and her sweet baby boy, Colin."

Annika noticed the sleeping infant in its baby carrier for the first time and smiled, as Devon continued, "And Sue, who owns Tasty Delights Bakery and Betty Watson." Then she added, "Annika is a podcaster, working on a new series while she's staying in Maple Glen."

"Cool," Sue said, as Betty simultaneously asked, "What's that?" and everyone laughed.

I think I'll be okay working with these ladies, Annika thought, taking a seat.

"Help yourselves, ladies," Devon said.

Annika realized they'd been waiting for her and was touched by the hospitality. Her next thought was that the overall welcoming in Maple Glen from everyone had been extraordinarily warm. The plates of treats, jugs of water and orange juice and an urn of coffee got her attention then and she hoped the other women couldn't hear her stomach rumble. She'd just poured herself a second cup of coffee when a loud rap on the front door startled her.

"That must be Sheriff Gallagher," Devon said with a laugh. "Maybe he's used to knocking on doors of some dubious types back in Boston."

"He can knock on my door anytime," quipped Betty, to more giggles.

Annika feigned interest in the refreshment table as Devon returned seconds later with Nate. She had her back to the room when he walked in behind Devon and could tell from their greetings that the women liked him, a fact she could understand, given his good looks and his confident demeanor. That pleased her, though she couldn't explain why. When she turned around, he was shaking hands with the other women and looking very handsome in his new khaki and forest-green uniform.

"And of course, you've met my sister, Annika," Devon was saying, diverting Annika's attention from Nate's uniform. "Help yourself to refreshments, Sheriff," Devon added.

"Um, Nate is fine by me. I'm not big on formalities, and just coffee will do, thanks."

"Sure." Devon picked up a mug and filled it from the urn. "How do you take it?"

"Black."

There was a bit of laughter as Annika and Nate replied as one, and she guessed any speculation from the women about her and Nate had now been confirmed. But once they were all seated, with Nate at the center of the table across from Annika, a businesslike tone prevailed.

"I've asked Betty to recap for you what Maple

Glen has done in other years for Halloween, because this is my first one here, too." Devon smiled pointedly at Nate, and then Annika. "We've already had a couple of organizing meetings and have decided to carry on previous traditions, though maybe some of us want to include some new ideas. Why don't you go ahead, Betty, while I make another pot of coffee?"

Annika was awed by the way Devon managed the information sharing before turning the meeting over to Nate. He had time to process all their thoughts and ideas, which Annika guessed Devon had intended, allowing an unhurried discussion afterward. The casual and friendly ambience was a sharp contrast to the public meeting on Sunday and Annika thought maybe her sister ought to run in the next election.

Betty summarized for Nate the events at the community center—the pumpkin carving contest, the face painting, costume contests and later, the teen dance—and when she sat down it was Nate's turn to speak.

He seemed about to stand, maybe forgetting he was at a casual get-together, but settled back into his chair. A rush of warmth swept through Annika, thinking he might be nervous, and she wanted to reassure him that everyone in the room was interested in what he had to say. Especially, her.

"Uh, thanks for inviting me to be part of the organizing committee for the Halloween celebrations in Maple Glen, although it seems you've already done most of the work," he began. "I've had active roles on other community committees in Boston and enjoyed working with people who cared about the places where they lived. I have that same feeling here, in Maple Glen, but in a more personal way. That's the benefit of living and working in a small town or village. Former Sheriff Anderson told me about the traditional Halloween parade and the decoration of the police cruiser, which I gather leads the parade. I'm hoping that some of the committee, or other Glen residents, will decorate the cruiser, because that's not my forte, to be honest."

"You'll be driving it, though, won't you Sheriff? Um, I mean, *Nate*?" Betty asked.

"Definitely. Halloween is on a Saturday this year but I'll technically be on duty, as I am now, so will be wearing my uniform."

"And a nice one, too," Betty interrupted.

Annika saw Nate's face redden and felt bad for him. She was about to say something to redirect the conversation when Devon spoke up. "We should also have the parade earlier on the Saturday because kids will be out trick-or-treating that evening."

"That sounds like a good plan," Nate said.

"Then I assume the cruiser decorating can take place on the Friday night. I can drive it to the community center parking lot, and it'll be all ready for the parade."

When everyone began talking at once, Devon clapped her hands and said, "Sounds like we all approve of your suggestion, Nate. We know you're on duty and need to get back to the station. Many thanks for coming."

There was a light round of clapping and Nate rose to leave. For a second he paused to look directly at Annika. She felt her face heat up and wondered if he was hinting that she go with him, perhaps to talk about last night or even ask about his plan to go to Wallingford that day. She was tempted to pipe up that it was time for her to leave too but figured the ploy would be too obvious, especially to the five women staring intently at Nate.

Instead, she peered down at her hands folded together on her lap, refusing to look his way, because everything she'd felt last night when he'd kissed her would be written on her face for all in the room to see. Afraid especially that the man who'd been in her mind all night long might see something else. That he was now also in her heart.

CHAPTER TEN

NATE SET THE GPS system in the cruiser to direct him to the Wallingford address on the Post-it note. His hand shook a little, either from too much caffeine without food, or from seeing Annika at the meeting that morning. He'd assumed she'd be there because they'd been drafted to the Halloween planning committee at the same time, but he'd figured if her night had been as sleepless as his, she might have skipped it.

She'd liked his uniform though. He'd seen her eyes widen and her face turn pink when he'd followed Devon into the dining room. Two clues that she might have been thinking of their kiss in the cruiser last night, just before the mystery car's headlights hit them. That interruption had been timely, because Nate wasn't sure where the fumbled kiss might have led. Nowhere good, he thought in the cold, hard light of a new day.

The meeting with the Bennington County Council about the parking permit issue was set for later that afternoon, which would give him plenty of time to check out the Wallingford address. He was about to drive away from the station lot when he spotted Shelley waving at him from the door. He shifted the cruiser into Park and rolled down the window.

"Just got a phone call from Captain McAllister," she was saying as she approached. "He says to tell you that someone has tampered with the blaze marks on the Trail, but that he and his volunteers will fix them so not to worry about that and also, he wants this to be added to the meeting's agenda today. The thing about the blaze marks, I mean. Whatever those are."

Nate took a second to respond. Eventually he'd become accustomed to Shelley's communication quirks but hoped he wouldn't miss some crucial information in the process. He, too, didn't know what blaze marks were, but guessed he'd soon find out. "Okay, thanks, Shelley. I'll give him a call after I see this woman in Wallingford."

"Great. Good luck, Nate. If anything else important comes up, I'll contact you by the radio set."

Nate nodded, rolled his window up and headed for Wallingford. The half-hour drive gave him a chance to go over what he'd do there, depending on the response of the woman whose car he'd sighted last night. He decided to set her at ease right away, as most people were on edge when police turned up unexpectedly on their doorsteps. He'd learned that the hard way, as a rookie in Boston. Smiles usually worked, and a calm demeanor implying nothing much was amiss. Just a routine inquiry. He knew his training would kick in, though he smiled at the instant reminder that his training had deserted him last night.

Back to that again, Gallagher? He sighed. *The only treatment for your current condition is avoidance. Repeat after me*, he told himself. *Avoiding Annika as much as possible is your only way out of this mess.* Except it was a cure best achieved in a bigger place than Maple Glen.

By the time he reached the turnoff to Wallingford, he'd managed to refocus his attention on the day's job. In fact, he was energized by the chance to do some real police work, the first since his swearing in days ago. Community liaison was part of his mandate as interim sheriff, but not his favorite role. So far, the only occasions his adrenaline had surged were when he was around Annika Morrison. *Back to her again! Oh boy, Gallagher, you do have it bad.*

The GPS directed him to a dead-end street in a new suburb on the outskirts of Wallingford. He parked out front, double-checking the address, and scanning the house before getting out of the cruiser. It seemed to be a typical new build, similar in design to others on the street. He thought about the old-style houses in Maple Glen and wondered if new constructions like the ones in this subdivision would eventually start appearing there, too. He hoped not, but knew the chances were likely.

He climbed out of the cruiser, locked it and pocketed the keys. He mounted three concrete steps leading to a small porch and rang the doorbell. Waited, then rang it again. Finally, he heard the sound of approaching footsteps, and the door was flung open.

A woman, mid-fifties he guessed, and wearing sweatpants and T-shirt greeted him with an extremely angry expression and an opened mouth about to snarl something. He took a small step back and waited for her to register his uniform.

Her mouth closed. "Uh, yes?"

"Agnes Wolchuk?"

"Yes." She glanced over his shoulder at the cruiser.

"I'm Sheriff Nate Gallagher, from Bennington County Police and current interim sheriff in Otter Valley."

She blinked. "Okay. Interim? Is that…uh…a real thing?"

"It is and I'm a real sheriff. I'm here to ask you a couple of questions. First—" Nate withdrew the Post-it with the license information "—is that your license plate number?" He showed her the note.

"Yes. Why? What's this about?" Her voice lowered and she peered at the houses on either side.

Worried about the neighbors, he wondered? "Nothing serious, I assure you. I'm following up on an investigation into an incident in Maple Glen the other night." When he noticed her hand tighten its grip on the edge of the door, Nate knew he was at the right place.

"Uh, where's Maple Glen?"

He almost laughed at her ingenuous expression. "Well, it's a village a few miles from here, along Route 7, and I have clocked your car—*this car*—" he emphasized, waving the Post-it in his hand "—in the vicinity of Maple Glen where other cars were vandalized Sunday night."

"Okay…and?"

"Were you driving your car Sunday night through Maple Glen and if so, did you happen to see anyone tampering with parked vehicles?"

She shook her head.

"Is it Miss or Mrs. Wolchuk, and can you answer the question aloud, please?"

"Um, it's Mrs. and no, I didn't see anyone tampering with cars."

"And what was your purpose for being in Maple Glen that night?"

"Does that have anything to do with what you said about the cars?"

It didn't really, but now he was curious about her caginess. "It may or may not." He let that sink in a second. "But you have every right to consult a lawyer and come to the police station outside Bennington to discuss this further, if you prefer."

"No, uh…that won't be necessary. I was driving through the village looking for my husband."

Nate definitely hadn't been expecting that answer. "Go on," he said.

"We have a travel agency business in Wallingford and are having a media blitz to make people aware of all the tourist attractions in the county, especially in Wallingford itself. We were at the public meeting on Sunday, when you spoke about the parking permit issue and saw that some locals were upset about it."

"And?" He had a suspicion where this was leading but wanted her to spell it out for him.

"My husband and I felt something more needed to be done about the issue, because our travel business would be affected, too, not just businesses in Maple Glen. We're worried about the loss of income from all this. If people can park for free in Maple Glen, they won't come to

Wallingford, and we just put together package deals for hiking the Long Trail here—hotel and a multiday free parking ticket for the Wallingford entry gate."

Exactly as he and Annika—well, he amended that—*mainly* Annika had suggested. "And so you decided to soap some windows to pass on your message?"

"No! We made up those fake parking tickets but then had an argument about going through with our idea. Stanley drove away in a huff, and I worried he was going to go ahead with it and get in trouble, so I followed him in my car to stop him. The windows were already soaped when we got to Maple Glen. And yes, we did put the flyers on the windshields, but that's all."

Now she seemed close to tears, but Nate didn't relent. "Then why did you return to the area again last night?"

The tears flowed. "Because I haven't seen Stanley since and…to be honest…he's been in a snit about this whole thing, and I was afraid he might do something more serious than print phony parking tickets."

"Something like what?"

"I don't know. I just want him to come home so I can tell him off to his face."

Sounded like a good idea, Nate was thinking,

though he was a bit concerned that the man was missing.

"Okay, Mrs. Wolchuk, I advise you to stay away from Maple Glen in the meantime and when your husband returns, please have him call me or else come and see me at the station." He handed her his card with the station landline, and his police registered cell phone number.

Once back in his cruiser, he took a moment to go over what Mrs. Wolchuk had told him. He had a strong sense that she'd been keeping something from him, but what? At least he'd taken some notes and would read them over at the station before having Shelley type them into an official report. That reminded him to give Shelley an update about his visit.

"Let me know if Mr. Wolchuk phones or comes into the station. I'm on my way back now."

"Okay," she said, "and a reminder about Captain McAllister."

"Thanks, Shelley. I'll contact him and again, if Mr. Wolchuk shows up…"

"I'll let you know."

When they disconnected, Nate called Bennington Police and asked to speak to Chief McNaught. They hadn't met yet, so he was obliged to explain who he was and why he'd been following up a possible mischief charge in Wallingford, which was under Bennington County's jurisdiction. He hoped the chief would be understanding and fortunately for him, he was. They agreed to get together after the council meeting.

Finn was next on his list, but his phone went to voicemail and Nate left a message saying he'd heard about the problem on the Trail, and perhaps they could plan strategy with Chief McNaught later that afternoon.

He was buzzing with adrenaline on the way back to the police station, feeling that at last he was doing some real police work, and his energy high spiked even more when he received a text from Annika as he drove into the station parking lot.

Can you come for supper tonight? Six? I microwave a mean lasagna.

The unexpected invite took a long moment to process. He sat in his cruiser to read it again. The day had been touch and go, but the evening suddenly looked promising with the chance to see Annika again. Despite his vow to keep some distance between them, he knew his heart was going to rule once again.

ANNIKA STARED AT Nate's thumbs-up emoji, which was kind of cute but also a tad silly coming from a police officer, and wondered if she'd been too hasty inviting him for supper after the other night. It seemed that no matter how determined she was to avoid the handsome sheriff, he continued to turn up on her doorstep. She laughed at herself. *At your invitation, Morrison.*

She had a few hours and decided rather than the frozen lasagna, something from Leni's farm shop would be more appealing. The walk would also give her a chance to figure out the impression she wanted to make. Whether to act as though nothing had happened at all last night in the car, or as if their kiss had been relatively unimportant. By the time she was walking to the farm shop, she'd decided that being herself was the best course of action.

Her plans fizzled when she arrived at the shop and saw the sign on the door. She hadn't noticed the store hours when she'd visited before, only now realizing the place closed at five on Mondays and Tuesdays. Probably due to its long weekend hours, she guessed. Well, lasagna it would be. She was walking back onto Church Street when she heard the beep of a car horn from behind, and swung around to see Devon behind the wheel, waving at her.

"Going my way?" she asked, rolling down her window.

"I was hoping to do some shopping at the farm

shop but just now found out it closes early on Mondays and Tuesdays."

"Yeah, Leni figured she needed family time more than shop time, especially after the longer weekend days. What were you hoping to buy? Maybe I can loan you something. We always seem to have a full pantry at the Manor."

Telling her would entail revealing that Nate was coming for supper, but Annika decided the village eyes would know soon enough anyway. "Um, I have a microwave lasagna at my place and decided to get something different at the farm shop but forgot about its hours." She knew from Devon's face—a mix of amusement and mystification—that she was babbling.

"Why don't you come and have supper with us, then?"

"Um, well, because I've invited Nate for six and he's probably already on his way back from Bennington."

Devon laughed. "You could both come."

"Thanks, but…uh…the thing is, I was hoping to have a private conversation with him." She saw the immediate rise of curiosity on her sister's face. "Nothing serious. Just…um… I'm hoping to get some advice, or ideas even, for my new podcast series. Legal ideas."

"I'm intrigued. Well, how about I give you a lift to your place—since it's right behind mine—

and on the way I can pop into my house and dig something out of the freezer or fridge for you to serve Nate."

Annika climbed into the passenger side and sagged against the seat. "Thanks, Devon. Saved by—"

"The bell, as the saying goes?"

Annika buckled up and Devon shifted the car into Drive. "No," she said, looking at Devon and smiling. "Saved by my older sister."

Devon took one hand from the steering wheel to give Annika's a quick squeeze, then took her foot off the brake and drove to the Manor.

Annika was relieved that Devon didn't fire questions about her and Nate having dinner together and figured that wasn't her sister's style. As someone who'd been the focus of much gossip and speculation, Devon had chosen to remove herself from the entire gossip web and Annika admired her for that decision.

Lately she'd been thinking about her former *We Reveal It* podcast series. The topic of revealing political corruption still appealed to her, and she was considering going back to it if Christine, her contact at Venture Media, didn't like her new pitch on local legends and folklore. She might even be able to connect that topic with a look at the grittier side of small-town life. The secrets. And she knew exactly where she could get the material. The Glen grapevine.

CHAPTER ELEVEN

NATE EXHALED A LONG, silent whoosh of air as the Bennington County Council approved a thirty-day parking permit reprieve for Maple Glen, with notices delivered by email or regular mail to residents informing them of the final decision. The permit decision itself would be reevaluated after that extension. One council member had suggested the implementation of a version of Neighborhood Watch as well, but after a very brief discussion that idea was squelched, to Nate's relief. The last thing he wanted was to have parking permit vigilantes patrolling the village.

The Wolchuks were responsible for the flyers, but Nate had yet to find the soaping perp. He smiled at his term, one that sounded less menacing than vandal, but the action still constituted a kind of vandalism. Not one that would hold up in court, he suspected, and neither would the flyers. Judges and attorneys were far too busy with real criminals, and he was grateful that the problem in Maple Glen hadn't escalated to that degree.

Another motion that was passed centered on Nate's budget and his request for office upgrades. He texted the news right away to Shelley and suggested she do some online browsing through office equipment sites. She'd responded with handclap and fireworks emojis, the latter reminding him that although the forecast for tonight was rain, clear night skies for the rest of the week were predicted.

He intended to ask Bernie about using the B and B roof for some stargazing while the Fireworks Galaxy was still going to be visible. Maybe Annika would be interested. He'd mention it at dinner—the microwave lasagna. Her text had made him smile as he thought back to the day they happened to meet at the grocery store in Wallingford with their shopping baskets filled with instant meals. If he was lucky, she might still have some of the ice cream she'd bought.

His thoughts had drifted to the flavors of ice cream she'd chosen when the chair of the council declared the meeting over and people got up to go to the refreshment table. Nate wasn't interested in hanging around the assembly room. He and Finn were meeting with Chief McNaught to talk about the specific issues of the soaping and fake flyers, and Nate planned to add in his thoughts on possible mischief charges against the Wolchuks. When he noticed Finn tilt his head to an exit to the hallway, Nate nodded and followed him, managing to evade a couple of people heading his way.

"Happy with the outcome?" Finn asked when Nate caught up to him.

"A month's reprieve will give all of us a chance to find out if permits are what the community wants. But I'm glad the notices will be sent from the council, and not the sheriff's office. I hope they include phone and email info for any further complaints."

Finn chuckled. "You said it! What're your plans now, before the meeting with Chief McNaught?"

"Go back to the station to finish up some paperwork and hopefully get an early night." He was still feeling the effects of last night's stakeout in his car, with the embarrassing memory of being caught sleeping on the job by Annika. To her credit, though, she'd brought coffee and hadn't teased him.

"Feel up to a side trip on the way back to the station?"

"What do you have in mind?"

"Thought I'd check out a small portion of the Trail, the access point near my house, and see what damage has been done to the blaze markers. Then I can figure out what equipment I'll need when my team of volunteers and I put them all back in place."

Nate immediately thought of Stanley Wolchuk. He hadn't received an update about the missing man from his wife, so assumed he hadn't gone home or was out on the Trail. Which, given the imminent rain, wasn't a good thing.

"I guess Shelley can hold the fort until closing time. She can contact me if anything pops up."

"Okay, but cell phone coverage on the Trail will be dicey."

Right. He hadn't considered that. Then he had an idea that amused him. "I'll ask her to contact Chief McNaught if there's a problem." He saw Finn's grin, and added, "Yeah, let's do it."

On the way to the parking lot, he gave Finn a brief summary about his visit to the Wolchuk home and the possibility that the man could be on the Trail.

"That doesn't sound good," Finn commented. "We need to determine if this guy is actually out there. Meet me at my place as soon as you get back to the Glen." He looked down at Nate's shoes. "If you have better footwear, make a quick change."

"Then our meeting with Chief McNaught is definitely off?"

Finn shrugged. "I think this constitutes a small emergency and meetings can always be rescheduled. I figured that out my first year as captain."

"Guess I should let him know." He took out his phone.

"Send him a text." Finn was grinning.

Nate was liking McAllister more and more and sent the text. Forty-five minutes later he was standing next to Finn on the bridge spanning Otter Creek. He'd left the cruiser parked in front of Finn and Devon's place—The Manor, as its faded and lopsided sign on the mailbox said—for easy access in case of emergency.

"Guess no one will give that a fake ticket," Finn quipped, pointing to the cruiser as he got out of his own car. He went round to the rear and opened the trunk, pulling out a large backpack.

"Yeah, I'm thinking the Glen has seen the last of those," Nate said. He glanced down at Finn's sturdy boots and hoped his new sneakers would be up to the hike. He'd taken the time to change into jeans and a sweatshirt, not wanting to risk any damage to his new uniform, and had the feeling the whole scenario—their unauthorized mission and his lack of a uniform—would raise an eyebrow from Chief McNaught. The fact that he didn't actually care was no surprise, because Nate had always chafed at following protocol.

"Look at this as an opportunity to get familiar with the locale," Finn said, as he came up to

Nate. "I'm sure Chief McNaught would approve. Or I should change that to 'reluctantly' approve."

Nate laughed. "I think you've already got a lead on my new boss."

"But only until the next election, right? When those of us here in Otter Valley are hoping *we* will be your new boss."

Nate was touched by the implied compliment, even though he sometimes doubted he'd be policing Maple Glen in a year's time. But returning to Boston wouldn't be an option. He'd burned his bridges there when he'd exposed the corruption in his precinct. Although he'd made friends in Maple Glen, he wondered if mere friendships would be enough for a future there. When he was younger, he'd been content with casual romantic relationships, but the last couple of years he'd felt a yearning for something more. Perhaps the change deep inside was due to his advancing age—okay, thirty definitely wasn't old—but generally at a certain time in a person's life, the desire for a more permanent, settled relationship kicked in.

"All right, so before we start out on the Trail, a couple of reminders," Finn was saying.

Real life brought Nate back to where he was and why. "Okay," he said.

"First, I'm leading the way because I know this part of the Appalachian like…like I know what kind of cake my mother will bake for my birthday. Chocolate fudge." He smiled at Nate's grin. "What I'm saying is that you stay behind me no matter what, and no drifting off the path for any reason."

Nate felt like an elementary student all over again, which he was compared to Finn's expertise and experience. He'd only lived in big cities and couldn't imagine "drifting" off a path in any woods or forest. The closest he'd ever come to wildlife had been routing raccoons and squirrels away from his urban garbage bin, and his only camp adventure as a kid had ended with tearful pleas to have his mother pick him up three days early.

"Lead on," he told Finn, giving him a salute.

Finn strapped on the backpack, gave a thumbs-up and stepped onto the bridge.

The first thing Nate noticed was the silence. He'd been waiting for birdsong or insects chirping, but the only sounds were the crunch of boots on the scatter of dead leaves across the flat slabs of rocks that composed the footpath. He amended the thought. Finn's boots were louder than Nate's rubber-soled sneakers. He risked a glance downward, noting that the nylon fabric over the toe sections was already wet. He focused on Finn's broad shoulders and the swaying backpack, while the discomfort inside him mounted with every footstep.

Finn abruptly came to a stop after what seemed hours to Nate, though a furtive peek at his phone told him they'd only been walking twenty minutes. He couldn't see exactly what had caught Finn's eye until he moved aside and noticed a piece of board hammered into a tree trunk about chest high—well, Finn's chest high, not Nate's—and on the board was a long rectangular streak of white paint.

"This is a blaze," Finn said, and tapped the board with an index finger. "It's basically a trail marker, and the kind we use on the Appalachian Trail. This part, anyway, because the Trail goes through many states and the blazes differ according to who's in charge of them."

"Like you?"

"I'm only a volunteer for search and rescue, and not responsible for blazing. The actual people in charge of ensuring the right markers are placed on the right paths and so on, are officials of the Trail Conservancy. There are lots of different colors signifying lots of different messages throughout the state, but here in this area, we have primarily white and blue blazes."

"Okay." Nate peered around but didn't notice any blues.

"The blue blazes mark paths that are off trail.

If someone wants to take a different route from the most common one to get somewhere in these woods, they'd follow the blue blazes."

"And are they like that?" Nate nodded his head to the painted board.

"Yep, only blue."

"I don't see how they can be tampered with."

"Someone could switch out the boards, move a blue one and hammer it on a different path. Or do the same thing with a white board."

"Misdirecting people then? Would that be serious?"

"It could be, for a novice hiker or someone who's not familiar with this section of the Trail. People could get lost or end up in a different location than they'd expected."

Nate thought about Stanley Wolchuk. Somehow, he couldn't envision him being so clever or quick thinking. He hadn't met the man but figured someone who'd assumed people would fall for the phony parking tickets might not have the know-how to fake or switch trail markers.

"I'm not sure the guy I'm looking for is capable of that," he said.

"Yeah, same here. Shall we go a bit farther until we find any that've been damaged?"

Nate shifted from one wet foot to the other and sighed. "Yep," he said, thinking wistfully of a hot shower followed by a hot cup of coffee. Even tea would do.

But a mere twenty minutes later, confirmed when Nate took another peek at his phone, Finn stopped again. He gestured to two side-by-side pieces of wood, one with a white streak of paint and the other, a blue. "See this?"

Nate did, and hoped Finn would explain it to him. "A hiker unfamiliar with this area would accept these as genuine."

"But?" Nate was feeling tired and hungry.

"They've been reversed."

"And?" He was picturing something like a grilled cheese sandwich after the coffee.

Finn's frown suggested Nate hadn't been listening. "They'll send us in the wrong direction!"

"Right." He was now worried that if he chose to turn around and leave, go home and relax, he wouldn't know which way to go.

Finn pulled a cell phone out of his jacket pocket and started taking pictures. "Did you bring yours?" he suddenly asked.

"Oh, yeah." Nate reached into the rear pocket of his jeans for his phone. He almost dropped it from his shaking hands but took a deep breath and pulled himself together.

After he'd snapped a few, Finn said, "Shall we go back now?"

Yes, Nate wanted to cry. Instead, he replied,

"What about Stanley Wolchuk? My missing suspect?"

"I doubt he's in these woods," Finn said.

His answer was almost condescending, and that irked, but Nate knew he wasn't in the best shape for interpreting nuances of tone or gesture. "What makes you think that?"

"Because I don't think a guy like the man you're looking for could do this." He waved at the tree with its blazes. "And I don't think that man could even get this far on his own."

Exasperation surfaced. "Then why have *we* come this far?"

"To see what's been done here. The vandalism of those blazes."

Blazes! Nate had the same thought, but it didn't pertain to tree markings. "Can we go back to Maple Glen, then?"

"Of course. Who's leading this time?"

He was joking of course, but Nate was feeling grumpy. "You are," he mumbled. He turned around and started following Finn, his mind shifting again to visions of a hot shower or beverage. Definitely a grilled cheese sandwich.

Luckily for Nate, they found Stanley ten minutes later.

ANNIKA HADN'T HEARD from Nate all day. He'd replied to her dinner invite with a thumbs-up, which made her think he'd been teasing her own use of emojis, and that made her smile. She knew he had a meeting with the Bennington County Council and guessed Finn might have also attended, therefore Devon might know something. But when she texted her sister, the reply was another emoji. Annika groaned, wanting more information than a tiny woman shrugging.

The weight of her new secret was almost unbearable. She could have told Devon, of course, but wanted Nate to be the first to learn that Venture Media was interested in her new podcast idea. He'd encouraged her from the beginning, even suggesting some kind of collaboration and although that idea hadn't panned out, she knew he'd be happy for her. Now she had a second chance with Venture, and her contact, Christine, urged her to send a sample episode as soon as possible.

She keyed in Devon's number and waited for it to ring out. At the voicemail prompt, she simply said she hadn't heard from Nate and wondered if Finn or Devon could pass on a message that Annika was expecting him at six. The important question she really wanted to ask was—*Do you know where Nate is?*

The answer came shortly after and Annika stared at the text for a long moment, heart thumping against her ribs and mouth dry. He's with Finn at the hospital.

Annika muttered as she wrote back, What's happened? The incoming words were slow and she was about to cancel and phone again when the message appeared.

Finn and Nate found a man injured on the Trail near our place and have taken him to the hospital.

Seconds later, another message.

Nate has arrested the man but has to stay at the hospital guarding him until Bennington Police arrive because they found a bag of money with the man. Finn passed on this info to me because Nate's phone is dead.

Annika's breathing returned to normal. When she read what Devon wrote next, she didn't know whether to laugh or cry.

Nate says to save him some lasagna.

CHAPTER TWELVE

NATE WAS ENJOYING his second serving of chili when Annika brought him another glass of sparkling water and plunked down on the sofa next to him. The bounce jiggled the water which sloshed a tiny bit into Nate's bowl, but he didn't care. It was delicious. Fortunately, she wasn't one of those people who talk to you while you're eating so he was able to wolf it down while it was still hot. Then he reached over to set his empty bowl on the small table beside him and drink some water.

"Thanks for supper, Annika. I was starving and I appreciate the change from lasagna to chili. I have to say, someone needs to redesign hospital vending machines." He sat back against fluffy cushions that, in his own house, he'd have tossed onto the floor and waited for her inevitable avalanche of questions.

She laughed and Nate thought how much nicer a sound it was than the slap of running and sliding footsteps still echoing in his head after he and Finn raced toward Stanley Wolchuk.

"How is your suspect? Or prisoner? Which is it?"

"Wolchuk's fine, resting in a hospital bed with a sprained ankle, along with some dehydration. However, an officer from Bennington is standing by there until he's discharged and Chief McNaught told me to take a couple of days to recuperate because Bennington will take over the case now. Wolchuk might be the person who tampered with the blaze markings, which could lead to a mischief charge."

"What if you hadn't found him? Or if something had happened to you or Finn?"

Nate was too exhausted to imagine the last scenario. "Finn would have been the only winner in that story. He knows those woods like… like he knows chocolate fudge cake. You had to be there," he added at her puzzled expression.

"Have you found out why the man was even out on the Trail, if he didn't tamper with those things you were telling me about?"

"The blazes. They're markers basically, pieces of wood with streaks of white or blue paint to show hikers which paths are which and which ones to take. Something like that." His mind was a bit fuzzy from fatigue but more from the woman next to him. Nate could barely hold his head up. He drank more water, spilling a bit as he set the glass back onto the table.

"I'm going to clear this stuff up, Nate. Why don't you lie down for a minute while I do that and then we can figure out how to get you home. Maybe Finn can help."

"No, no. Finn has had a worse day than I have, believe me. After we found Stanley, I fell and hit my head, which is why my clothes were all muddy, and why Finn gave me some of his instead so Devon could wash mine, and they brought me here so you could keep an eye on me."

She didn't laugh this time. "They didn't want you to be alone, and I volunteered."

"Aw, thanks." He leaned his head against the back of the sofa and closed his eyes. It had been a long day, and it was finally over.

WARMTH, AND FAMILIAR AROMAS—coffee?—registered first, then shafts of sunlight across his chest and legs. Nate turned his head on the pillow and realized he was still in Annika's living room on her sofa and covered by a blanket. Not on the Trail. Not in a hospital room. Relief seeped out of him. Everything was okay. He was okay. Finn was definitely okay. Stanley Wolchuk… He wasn't quite so certain about him, but hoped the man was okay, because he intended to testify at his trial. He swung his legs onto the floor and sat up, waited for a slight dizziness to settle, and then stood.

Annika appeared with a tray of food. "Do you want to eat on the sofa, or at the table?"

"The table, I think. Less problematic." He inhaled slowly, then wobbled toward the dining area near the galley kitchen. He wasn't a fan of an open plan design, but it worked here, creating a brighter effect than smaller rooms would.

She went ahead of him and placed the contents of the tray onto the table. He was relieved to see toast, what looked like scrambled eggs, and a mug of coffee. His stomach rumbled as he sat, and he caught her smiling. "Thanks, Annika. This looks great." He noticed the mug of coffee at her place as he sat down. "You're not eating?"

"I'm not a breakfast person," she said, settling onto her chair.

He focused on the food then, trying to eat slowly, despite his stomach urging otherwise. Three sips of coffee and he was ready to take on the world. Or at least Annika's questions, which came almost immediately.

"What was the reason for that man—Stanley?—placing all those fake tickets on the cars?"

"You suggested a reason that same day. To protest the parked cars."

"Okay, but Finn told Devon that Stanley lived

in Wallingford. Why would he care about the street parking here in Maple Glen?"

"His aim was to discourage tourists from even coming to the Glen. If they couldn't park and access the Trail here, they'd have to go to Wallingford." He paused to swallow a mouthful of egg. "Stanley and his wife own a travel business in Wallingford with package deals for hiking the Trail, but from the entry gate there."

"That still doesn't make sense. The permits here will be temporary. Didn't the council approve only a thirty-day extension for them?"

"Right, but apparently the Wolchuks owe money everywhere. I guess Stanley felt they couldn't wait."

"If they owe money, what was Stanley doing with a bag of it?"

"Okay, so poor old Stanley clearly wasn't thinking straight in all this. He cleaned out the joint bank account with his wife and headed for the Trail. His plan was to bury it and then abscond."

"Abscond?"

Nate grinned at her expression. "Yeah, I don't get a chance to use that word very often, but it fits the situation. He'd embezzled from his own business and was going to run away with the money, but at the last minute, I think he was filled with guilt about doing a number on his wife. Then he decided to bury the money and stage a fake robbery at their business. That way he might have had some kind of insurance payback and still would have the embezzled money hidden on the Trail."

Annika frowned. "He doesn't sound very bright. I mean, he could have buried that money in his own backyard. Or any place other than the Trail."

"True. And he wouldn't have fallen and sprained his ankle, allowing us to find him. I think he got the idea the night they put the fake tickets on cars and he figured no one—neither his wife, nor the police if she contacted them—would think he'd hide the money on the Trail."

"Then how does the wife fit into this scam?"

"I think she honestly didn't know about any of it and I'm betting Stanley wasn't planning to take her with him."

"I hope he goes to jail," she muttered.

"The embezzlement charge will certainly lead to jail time." Nate set his fork down after he finished off the rest of his breakfast.

"Good," she murmured. She sipped some coffee, then plunked her mug down on the table.

Nate sensed something else was on her mind. "You have news?"

"I do. I'd planned to tell you sooner, but then the incident on the Trail with Stanley and everything was…well…a big distraction. To say the least."

She bit her lip and Nate realized that she'd been worried about him. The notion warmed him, knowing she'd cared enough to be anxious. He was about to say something when her face lit up.

"Venture Media is willing to look at my new idea, about legends and folklore in small town America."

"Hey! That's fabulous." He shoved his chair back and went to her, wrapping his arms around her in a long hug. Her eyes were shining when he pulled away. "You must be over the moon."

"Overwhelmed actually. I've only written one episode, and they want it as soon as possible."

"You can do it," Nate said, looking down at her. "I'm sure you already have those other episodes in mind."

"I do, though I'm also hoping I can eventually convince them to buy my other series, too. The one about small-town corruption. I plan to keep working on it, at the same time."

"So what's the episode after the Champy one?"

"We have kind of a legend right here in Maple Glen and I thought I'd start with him. Local and relatively current."

Nate felt a prickle of unease. "Who's that?"

"His name is Walter Ingram, and I'd really like you to come with me for moral support when I pitch the idea to him."

The churning in Nate's stomach returned with a vengeance. "I can't imagine you needing moral support, Annika." He aimed for a tease, hoping to get out of accompanying her, until he saw the disappointment in her face and mumbled, "Sure."

But was he sure? Not at all. Yet one thought finally emerged. This wasn't what he'd planned days ago, when he first arrived in Maple Glen, but at least he'd be meeting Walter Ingram with another person at his side. Buffers were always good to have in potentially emotional situations.

ANNIKA KEPT GLANCING at Nate's fingertips drumming on the steering wheel on the way to Walter's. Something was on his mind, and she didn't think it was connected to what had happened yesterday, because these new signs of stress hadn't appeared until she'd asked him to go with her to interview Walter.

She herself had been floating all morning on the memory of last night—talking and laughing with him about the strange day, until he'd rested his head against the back of the sofa and had fallen asleep. She'd covered him with a comforter, wishing that she could lie down beside him and let the world outside disappear.

For now, though, she was heading for an interview that she hoped would be podcast worthy and with an actual hero whom she'd known about for months but was meeting for the first time. A legend, and the focus of her second podcast. Now that Venture Media was open to considering her new idea, she figured an interview with Walter, a living local hero and legend, would sweeten the deal even more. Perhaps enough to go for more money before she signed the actual contract.

"You turn here," she told Nate as the sign indicating Route 7 appeared ahead. But he'd already clicked on the turn signal, and she realized he knew where he was going. They traveled a short distance along the county road and then Nate slowed down, looking to his right, the far side of the road. When a large house with a sign that read Walter's Honey appeared on a small crest of hill, he clicked on the blinker again and turned onto the gravel driveway, continuing to its very end at a long, low concrete building. A pickup truck was parked close to the building's door and next to it, a sedan. Nate braked, shifted into Park and turned off the engine.

When he sat without moving, Annika asked, "Is everything okay?"

"Yep," he said, but didn't turn her way.

She saw that he was staring at the building, as if deciding his next move. "You can wait for me in the car, if you'd rather."

When he didn't answer, she was about to ask him if there was a problem, but just then the front door of the building opened and a woman came out. Annika recognized her right away. Amelia Owens, the social worker who'd been assigned to Devon's case years ago. The woman whose careful and thoughtful investigations had led to the discovery of Blake Morrison's letter and from there, to Annika and Devon meeting for the first time. Annika flung open the car door and ran to hug her.

She was still embracing her when Walter Ingram appeared. At least, Annika assumed the tall man with steel-gray hair was Walter. He was using a cane and staring at the two women with a perplexed, but curious expression. When Annika let go of Amelia, the older woman turned around, dabbing at her eyes, to smile at Walter.

"This is Annika! Devon's half-sister."

Walter beamed and limped toward them. "Good gracious, what a surprise! When did you arrive in these parts?"

"A few days ago," she said.

"This calls for a celebration," he said. "Let's go into the house so you can tell us all your news." He turned to Amelia. "Can you stay a bit longer?"

"Of course."

Annika was thankful for that, sensing the woman would help ease the conversation. Then she remembered Nate. He was still in the car, staring though the windshield. She beckoned to him, but when he didn't make a move, she went to the driver's side window and tapped on it.

"Come and meet Walter and Amelia."

He nodded, keeping his eyes a minute longer on the two people ahead. Seconds before Annika was about to wrench open the door, he climbed out.

Something in his face prompted her to reach for his hand. "This is my friend, Nate Gallagher," she said, as she led him toward Walter and Amelia.

CHAPTER THIRTEEN

HIS GRIP BELIED the need for a cane, was Nate's first thought, and an indication that despite the hip, the man was hale and hearty. The twinkle in the gray-blue eyes suggested that Walter had already leaped to an assumption about the true nature of Nate's relationship with Annika, though he guessed that might be his imagination.

"You're the new sheriff here," Walter commented after the handshake.

His eyes narrowed. Appraising him, Nate wondered? "Yes, sir, I am."

"Well, come inside, you two," Walter went on to say. "We'll put the kettle on."

Nate was relieved that he'd clearly included Amelia. The more people present to hold and carry on a conversation, the better. Walter led the way through a side door of the house, with the two women following. Nate hung back, noting every detail of the dimly lit entry hall: the handmade wooden hooks just inside the door, the flocked wallpaper from a long-ago era and the large floor beams, polished by many footsteps over the years. Tall bookshelves lined one side of the hall, also handmade, and were overfilled with books, some lying on top of others. Another set of shelves was topped with carvings of birds, none of which Nate could identify, having seen mainly pigeons, sparrows and the occasional crow in his city upbringing.

The hall ended in a bright kitchen that surprised Nate with a cheerfulness absent from the entryway. Pale gray walls looked freshly painted and the white appliances surrounding the large wood table seemed fairly new. He watched while Walter eased himself into a chair and hooked his cane over the back of the one next to him.

"I'll get the kettle on," Amelia said, as she draped her sweater over a chair, "or would you people prefer coffee?"

Or something even stronger, Nate was thinking, but Annika replied for both of them. "Tea would be wonderful, thanks, Amelia."

Nate was suddenly curious about the house, and how long Walter had been living in it. Before, or after he'd met Nate's mother? He quelled the rush of questions. All in due time. He sat down and gazed around the room, noticing the small paintings on the walls and even a few painted wood-carved fish, that he also couldn't identify, his only experience with fish being at a favorite restaurant in Boston. When he turned his attention back to Walter, he saw a hint of curiosity in the man's eyes.

"Did you carve all these?" Nate asked, gesturing to the fish on the walls and the birds on the shelving unit near the entrance to the kitchen.

"I did, but many years ago, before the arthritis got into my hands." He tilted his head at the cane. "Had a hip replacement about six weeks ago."

"Oh? I…uh… I'm sorry to hear that."

"Well, don't be. My new hip is better than ever and so far—" Walter tapped the table "—my knees are in good shape." He seemed about to add something but paused as Amelia set a tray down on the table.

Nate eyed the cups, milk, sugar and jar of honey, lingering a bit longer on the plate of cookies. Homemade, judging from their crisped edges and their lack of factory uniformity. He was already liking Amelia.

When tea had been poured and cookies passed around, Walter asked, "How're you liking your posting, then?"

"It's only been a week, but I'm gradually getting used to things—the station and the parameters of the job. Also, the issues here that I'll be dealing with."

Walter snorted. "Hah! Good luck with the issues. I was at the meeting last Sunday, when folks got in a tizzy about parking." He paused to sip some tea. "Thought you handled them okay. Shied away from making promises you probably knew you couldn't keep."

Nate reached for a cookie and bit into it, enjoying the first bite when Walter asked, "Think you'll be able to stick around Maple Glen until the election next year?"

Nate took a second to swallow. "I hope so, sir. Everyone's been very hospitable and I'm already getting used to the rhythm of the place, if you know what I mean."

"That's a good word. Here in the Glen, life sways to some kind of rhythm for sure, and most people like that. They don't want things to change." Walter drank more tea, then seemed to be mulling over what he'd just said.

Nate waited, helping himself to another cookie. He noticed Amelia checking her cell phone and then he glanced to the end of the table where Annika was sitting and wondered why she was so quiet. When was she going to mention the interview? Wasn't that why she'd wanted to come?

"I heard about the car soaping and those flyers on the windshields," Walter finally said, with a loud tsk. "Have you arrested anyone yet? Cause that sounds like the kind of mischief people here don't like."

"Bennington Police and I are working on that." He knew better than to discuss a case before it came to trial. He'd already told Annika too much about Stanley but attributed his lapse to adrenaline and the aftereffects of the chase.

"The sooner the better. The damage was done here in Maple Glen and law enforcement here should be handling the case."

Amelia looked up from her phone. "Walter, there's no point going on about this. Nate and his colleagues are doing their best." She smiled at Nate, and then Annika. "I need to go, because my goddaughter is having a dance recital later this afternoon in Burlington." She reached for her sweater as she stood up. "Annika, I'm so happy you and Devon got together and wish you both all the best. If you ever want to talk about what happened years ago, please let me know. Devon has my email address."

After she left the room, Nate looked at Annika and tilted his head to Walter.

She got the message. "Walter, I'm working on a podcast series about American folklore and legends."

Nate hid a smile at Walter's expression, a mix of puzzlement and curiosity.

"A podcast! Gotta say I've heard of those but never actually listened to one. Tell me more."

"Well, the series is for a company called

Venture Media and if they buy it, it'll be aired widely."

"Sounds interesting."

Annika looked from Walter to Nate. Seeking encouragement, he wondered? He managed a slight shrug, now wishing he'd let her come by herself. The whole situation seemed so awkward.

"Well, I'd like to interview you, actually, for one of my episodes. As a local legend."

The interest in Walter's face vanished. "Nope."

Blunt and to the point. Nate admired that, but hoped Walter wouldn't be as quick to judge when Nate revealed his relationship to the man.

"It won't be the story about Devon. I'd never write her personal story, but the company is interested in my idea to write about local heroes and legends, and I'd love to interview you about any folktales or legends you personally have heard during your time here in Maple Glen."

"Except I haven't lived in the Glen all my life. I only moved here after..."

"After?"

"After I retired."

"When was that?"

"About twenty-five years ago."

"Before or after you found my sister, when she was missing on the Trail?"

"After."

Getting information out of the man was a

challenge. He clearly didn't want to talk about the incident that ended in too much media attention, and Nate doubted an interview was going to happen.

Walter himself must have been tiring of the questions, because he heaved a loud sigh and said, "Look, I'm no legend, believe me. I haven't heard any tales about strange events in this area, if that's what you mean by folklore. Tales that aren't always true but were carried down through generations, right?"

"Exactly!" Annika exclaimed. "Throughout history people have made up these stories, at first orally, and then in writing. They were passed down, and often altered through generations, but people are still attracted to them."

"Then you should talk to people who've lived here longer than I have. Like Bernie Watson, or Marion McAllister."

Nate saw the disappointment in her face. He guessed she was beginning to accept the fact that Walter either didn't intend to yield or had nothing to say on the subject, and part of him admired the man for that, because Annika Morrison was a force to be reckoned with. At the same time, he admired her, too, for that very persistence.

The quiet room was a big hint that it was time to leave, although Nate didn't feel ready to leave.

Not that he planned to reveal himself then and there. He didn't want another person with him when he did, because he couldn't trust his own emotions.

Would he be angry when he confronted the man with memories of the woman—Nate's mother—who'd clearly loved Walter at some point in her life? Who'd remained stoic in the last year of her life while encouraging Nate to find happiness and most of all, love. She'd been proud of his success in his police career yet wanted something more for him. Nate had always known what that was—someone to love, perhaps have a family with—but hadn't dreamed it would be a possibility.

Annika barely spoke on the drive back. Walter had given them each a jar of honey as they were leaving, to sweeten the disappointment of not getting an interview, Nate guessed. The outing had been a letdown for her, but satisfying for him. He'd learned a lot about Walter Ingram—his father. The man seemed curt, but honest; modest about his rescue of the Morrison children all those years ago and scrupulous about protecting their privacy, even now, twenty-five years later.

Nate had liked him, which was a good omen for the success of his mission in Maple Glen. Today wasn't the moment, but he wouldn't leave the town without telling Walter Ingram that he had a son, and that the son was Sheriff Gallagher. What happened afterward, Nate would leave to fate. Or karma. Or simply luck. Until then, he'd do his best for the people of Maple Glen.

ANNIKA COULDN'T RESIST frequent side glances at Nate on the way back to Maple Glen. She'd failed to secure an interview with Walter Ingram and was grateful for Nate's silence about it. Even the fact that he hadn't tried to cheer her up pleased her, because she loathed those kinds of half-hearted gestures.

What was on her mind though, was that very silence. He was clearly lost in thought, the way his eyes were glued to the road ahead, and his hands clenched on the steering wheel. After last night's talk and brief moment of togetherness, he was suddenly distant, and she had a feeling he was keeping something from her.

Moments like this were why she hadn't regretted leaving her last serious relationship, almost a year before Devon's wedding invite. She'd almost forgotten that time in her life until now, when she recalled some of her pointless introspection afterward. Her mother had once told her, after a tearful account of a college breakup, that there'd be other men in her life and better ones. Annika had eventually seen the truth in the consolation. Now she wondered what her mother would think of Nate and decided that, given Annika's obvious happiness, she'd like him.

"What is it?"

Nate's unexpected question took a moment to register and when she didn't reply right away, he turned his attention from driving to her.

"You seem lost in thought," he clarified.

More like lost in the past, but she wasn't about to resurrect those years with Nate. "I was wondering why Walter was so adamant about not granting me an interview," she said, jumping to the second thing that had been on her mind. "I mean, why would he object to being equated with a folk legend? Even a modern-day one."

"Maybe he doesn't think of himself as heroic. He was a volunteer searcher back then and fortunately, made the decision to hand over the kids to the Department for Children and Families rather than return them to the foster parents."

"I guess you learned all that from the internet?" she asked.

"Yep."

"Does the online info match your impression of him, after meeting him in real life?"

"Online stuff is superficial. You can't determine a person's true character from data," he replied. "He strikes me as someone who values his privacy, and I imagine he lost quite a lot of that back then, with the media frenzy."

"Probably a reason, too, why Devon never talks about that time."

"Some things are best left in the past."

The tone in his comment almost sounded like a warning and she felt a rise of annoyance. As a journalist, she'd had plenty of doors closed in her face over the years, and Walter's refusal was merely one more. If she'd been discouraged by those past disappointments, she'd never have persevered with her eventual career change to podcasting.

"But Walter and Devon's story is old news," she pointed out.

"Not when you realize they only found each other shortly after last Christmas, and I bet not everyone in Maple Glen knows all the facts, in spite of that gossip thread."

"The grapevine? I love that term. Finn's mother told me a bit about it. She said although people here pass information around, the gossip is good-natured, not malevolent. In fact, I bet someone could use the grapevine to gather information, rather than spread it."

"What do you mean?"

Her thoughts raced ahead of her, and she took a minute to corral them. "If someone wanted to find out something, a way to do that would be to pass on a false bit of information."

"I hope you're not thinking of doing that." The car weaved slightly as he looked her way.

"Oh…uh…heaven's no. But I've been thinking about you and Finn finding those blaze markers, the ones that were mixed up and reversed. Stanley Wolchuk got lost because he was fooled by the switching of the blaze markers. What if whoever did switch them wanted to plant false information in the minds of people here? Instead of just making people get lost while hiking, someone was sending a different message."

He considered the idea for a long moment. "An interesting take on it, I have to admit. Especially if the switching of markers isn't connected to the car soaping. On the other hand, there's no evidence to lead to that conclusion."

No evidence yet, she was thinking. When they reached the end of the driveway leading to her cottage, she asked, "Would you like to come in for another coffee or even an early lunch?"

"Thanks, but it's still a workday for me. Shelley's been running the station on her own so…"

"I guess this outing to see Walter was—"

"Work. Exactly."

And that was that. She climbed out of the car and leaned down to say, "Thanks again, Nate, and guess I'll see you when we help you decorate your cruiser, for the Halloween parade on Saturday." She closed the car door and felt a brief rise of satisfaction at the unhappy expression on his face at her reminder.

CHAPTER FOURTEEN

NATE KNEW HE'D had an opportunity to tell Annika about his connection to Walter, and a part of him had wanted to do so. But she was a podcaster with a journalist's instinct for a good story. He didn't want his past to be material for a podcast listened to by thousands of people. That horrifying thought circled him back to Walter. Nate could totally identify with what the man must have been feeling as Annika had pitched her proposal. A strong desire for privacy was something he and Walter had in common, and Nate was beginning to wonder if Annika could accept that or even understand it. Persistence was her forte, after all.

When he reported for work the next morning, he noticed another car next to Shelley's and hoped it didn't belong to Chief McNaught, arriving unexpectedly to check up on him after the brush-off yesterday. But it was Shelley who met him at the front door.

"Sheriff Gallagher... Nate... I'm sorry to say this, but someone here needs to speak to you."

As she moved aside, Nate saw two people—a man and an older teenager—standing near her desk. The teen—male, about sixteen or seventeen, Nate was guessing—shuffled nervously and peered down at the floor. The fifty-something man looked embarrassed, and Nate noticed him glancing almost sheepishly at Shelley as she stood, arms folded, in the center of the room.

Nate set his cap down on Shelley's desk. "What's the problem?"

"This here is my ex, George, and my son, Jason. He has something to tell you."

Nate refrained from shaking hands with them, sensing this wasn't a friendly meeting. He nodded and said, "Okay. Go ahead, Jason."

The youth cleared his throat and when he spoke, his voice cracked.

From nervousness or puberty? Nate couldn't be sure, but he waited patiently.

"So...uh... I was the one who soaped those car windows."

Nate took in the red face and hunched shoulders. He was definitely afraid, which redeemed him a tiny bit in Nate's estimation. "And your reason for doing so?" he asked.

His quick shrug was followed by more throat clearing, this time from Shelley.

"No reason. I was just feeling angry and um… was ranting to my friends one night and they dared me to do something to kind of blow off steam without actually breaking the law and that's when I got the idea."

Nate took his time processing the confession while observing the genuine regret in the boy's face as well as the unhappiness in his parents'. "I see," he finally said, "but the problem is, the soaping was an act of mischief—a chargeable offense here in Vermont. People were very inconvenienced by it. I was called to investigate and subsequently filed an official report."

Tears welled in the teen's eyes. Nate saw the alarm in Shelley's face, but even though she was clearly upset, she didn't protest, and he respected her for that.

"What's the punishment for that?" asked George.

"Usually, a fine. Maybe some kind of restitution."

"So now what?" George asked.

"I think there may be more to the situation than Jason's letting on," Nate commented. When he saw the boy's face, he knew he was on the right track. "Not simply a dare from friends, right Jason?" The tears flowed now but he nodded, and Nate waited, giving the kid the time he needed.

"Mom and Dad split up a few months ago."

It wasn't the opening Nate expected, and he refrained from glancing at Shelley. "Go on."

"My brother and I had the choice to be with Dad in Burlington or stay at home with Mom, in Wallingford. We didn't want to change schools, so we chose that. Staying in Wallingford. But we felt guilty too, because we knew Dad would be alone and that wasn't fair." He looked at his father, who kept his eyes on the floor.

Hiding his own emotion, Nate thought. After a moment, Nate quietly asked, "But why soap car windows in Maple Glen? I'm not getting the connection."

"I was just… I don't know…angry and I knew Mom really liked working at the station, but I hoped if she thought this area wasn't a good place for kids—especially teenagers—because it's so small and nothing much happens here… she'd let us live with Dad."

Nothing much, except some minor vandalism, Nate thought. He steadied his breathing while mentally sorting out his options. The fact that no one was begging him to let the kid off the hook influenced the decision he finally made. He figured he had a certain amount of discretion and, regardless of what Chief McNaught might advise, he opted to trust his judgment.

"All right," he said, "here's what I'm going to do."

All eyes turned his way, but no one spoke.

Nate figured he was risking something at that point, maybe his job. But he'd made a few similar decisions while he was on the force in Boston and had never regretted them. Not even when some had led to verbal reprimands.

"This is only advice," he clarified, "but I strongly recommend all of you follow it. First, Jason must apologize in person to all the owners of the relevant cars. There were ten in all, and I have the names and addresses of the owners. If those owners aren't satisfied with an apology, then I may have to consider an official charge." He let that sink in.

"Okay," Jason said.

The fact that the kid didn't protest or show any sign of self-pity impressed Nate. He respected people who owned up to their faults or misdeeds. "Secondly, I advise that all of you—including the son who's not here today—come to a mutual agreement about who is living with whom, where and for how long. I recommend you two—" he looked at George and Shelley "—get some legal counseling about your separation, and also social counseling for the whole family. I know someone who might help you with the latter, if you're interested."

He let that register. "Finally, I suggest you give Jason some kind of curfew which he must keep. If he doesn't, I want you to let me know immediately, because then I'll have to reevaluate my decision." He saw from their faces that he didn't need to explain further. He knew he was taking a chance with his unorthodox suggestions, but he had a gut feeling that Jason wouldn't reoffend.

"Thank you, Sheriff," Shelley said.

They all looked exhausted, Nate thought. Stress and emotion did that to you, and for a second he went back to the morning and how he and Annika had parted. His feelings after the meeting with Walter Ingram had played a significant part in the way he'd responded with silence to Annika's attempts to reach out to him on the drive back to Maple Glen. He'd ignored her gesture, used to handling emotions on his own. His Boston experience after exposing minor corruption in his precinct had left him with a strong wariness about the media.

He suddenly realized the Barnetts were waiting for him to say something more. "Why don't all of you take some time this afternoon to go over everything I've said. Make some plans. Talk to one another."

"Thank you, Nate," Shelley said, dabbing at her eyes with a tissue.

As he watched them leave, Nate thought perhaps he ought to take his own advice. See Annika. Talk to her. Make some plans. Set some boundaries so that he could enjoy her company and get to know her better without worrying about potential conflicts arising from their work.

THE TEXT FROM DEVON, minutes after Nate had dropped Annika off, arrived exactly when she was desperate for a diversion.

Are you free for a final Halloween committee meeting at my place, this afternoon? Just tying up loose ends.

Never in a million years would Annika have been so thrilled at the prospect of a committee meeting. Her fingers practically flew over her phone keypad, and she wrote she was available to come right then. Devon took a few seconds longer to reply, *sure*. Annika needed company and discussing plans for a Halloween event that she didn't care about would suffice. And there was still the long, lonely night ahead to endure, replaying the uncomfortable ride home.

Yet the truth was, she'd been relieved that they hadn't discussed the meeting with Walter on the way back. Her frustration about all of it might have led to words she'd regret. That was her pattern. Blurting out whatever was on her mind—such as her intention to go ahead anyway with a podcast about a local hero. No names needed to be mentioned, simply a general talk on what constituted a legend with a summation something like…*modern day legends can simply be ordinary people who do something extraordinary, even just once in their lifetime.* The problem was Venture Media might not be so interested if her podcast subject was anonymous.

She reached for her cell phone to record the line about modern day legends while the words were still fresh, and then headed for Devon's. The front door had been left ajar, and the same group of women were gathered in the dining room when Annika walked in. She felt a brief disappointment at the lack of refreshments and concluded this really was last-minute. She slipped onto a chair, nodding at Devon, who was speaking to the rest of the committee, now familiar to Annika—Betty, Sue, Leni and Maura. The only missing person was Maura's baby, and Annika was struck by a second and unexpected letdown. Not that she was interested in, much less charmed by, the whole maternal thing. Domestic bliss relied heavily on the right combination of personalities and character, something Annika had learned growing up. Still, the baby was adorable.

Her parents had been happy together and she'd had an easy childhood until she was fifteen, when her father had died and his past had been revealed. She and her mother were still adjusting to that shock, though Annika now knew her acceptance of his secret had been made easier by connecting to Devon. She'd gone from being an only child to having a sibling in less than a year and was still dealing with all the emotional ups and downs involved.

"Thanks for coming at the last minute, ladies," Devon was saying, "but I thought we should have a brief rundown of events for Friday and, of course, Saturday. This is what I have so far. Leni is organizing the pumpkin carving contest. How's that going, Leni?"

"The notice of events on the flyer specified that people needed to provide their own pumpkins, which had to be carved ahead of time. The pumpkins will be displayed on a table inside the center, and each entry will have a number, rather than a name."

"Aw, I was planning to vote for my daughter's entry," Betty complained, adding at the chuckles, "Just kidding."

"Next," Devon went on, "is Maura, who's organizing the children's costume parade. What time is that and where will it happen?"

"My helpers and I thought the kids would like

to be in the actual parade this year, instead of just marching around the community center," Maura said. "And there won't be any judging, because we prefer not to highlight some costumes above others because...uh...they're kids."

"How will the parade itself work?" Devon asked.

"Sheriff Gallagher's cruiser is leading it, and walking behind will be some local politicians and business owners from Wallingford and beyond. Many of them sponsored the events so we thought they should be recognized," Maura said.

"Good idea," Devon said. "And it starts at—"

"Ten. We put that time on the flyers we mailed out a week ago, and I think we can safely stick with that, unless something unexpected happens. Also, the teen dance is planned for tomorrow night, rather than Saturday."

"Okay, thanks, Maura, and just to let all of you know," Devon continued, "the cruiser decorating is still on for tomorrow at the end of the day so any kids can come and help. I've texted Sheriff Gallagher a reminder and he suggested we do it in the community center parking lot. The car can remain there until the parade kicks off. He's also asked for some reinforcements from the Bennington Police Department to make sure no one parks on Church Street the night before, to keep it clear for the parade. He told us that

Sheriff Anderson had already applied for the parade permit, so we don't have to worry about that. The decorations used in the past are in a locker at the police station."

Nate hadn't passed on any of this to Annika, which gave her some insight into what life might be like being married to a police officer. Information sharing could definitely be limited. The idea saddened her a bit, especially regarding her podcast plan. She worried that going ahead with her new idea could jeopardize her chance of a future with the sheriff but knew she had to take that risk. He hadn't been enthused about her plan to interview Walter as a local legend, but getting a contract for her new series meant paying off debts and even more, establishing a recognized name for herself in the podcast business.

Devon's voice brought Annika back to the meeting, and away from Nate Gallagher.

"Sue, your turn."

"Okay, we know where and when the cruiser decorating happens, but which of us are actually going to be in charge of it? Because my staff and I will be busy all day baking Halloween cookies and making pumpkin pies and tarts," Sue said.

"Right and I figured that. Any volunteers for the decorating?" Devon looked at the group.

"Theo has to work at the clinic and it's a school day, so my regular babysitters—Luke and Ashley—won't be available until after four o'clock, when the bus brings them back from Rutland," Maura said. "I may have to bow out, but I think the kids will want to help."

"Ashley definitely wants to participate when she gets home from school, and there's a chance my son, Scott, may take the weekend off from his studies to come home for the events. He mentioned it last time we spoke. I'll find out for sure tonight," Betty added.

"I can help," Leni said. "I've decided to close shop early on the Saturday because of the parade and I know Max and Emma will want to help with the cruiser decorating when they get home from school tomorrow."

"Nate did say he'd be available to help, too, barring any callout from the station," Devon added.

That bit interested Annika, as he hadn't looked thrilled when she reminded him about the decorating. All part of the community aspect of his job, she thought. "Uh…well… I can help with the decorating too," she said.

"Great. Okay, what's next on the agenda, ladies?" Devon asked.

"This hasn't anything to do with the parade," Betty said, "but does anyone know who was responsible for the car soaping? I don't like to think the person was someone from Maple Glen."

There was a collective shrug. Annika was glad she didn't know the answer to that question either, fearing her face could give it away. Nate had been wise not to share police information with her.

"And what about the mix-up with the markers on the Trail?" Betty persisted. "I heard about that from Bernie."

Annika's ears perked up. Of course, Bernie Watson must be related in some way to Betty Watson. She'd find out how later but for now, she wanted to know what Bernie knew about the blazes. "How did Bernie hear about it?"

"Maybe from someone staying at the B and B. His customers often go hiking."

"Is Bernie related to you?" Annika asked out of curiosity.

"My husband, Ed, is Bernie's brother."

"Well, whatever happens I'm sure we'll all be informed eventually," Devon said. "Either officially, from Bennington Police, or unofficially, through the grapevine."

It was clear Devon was putting an end to further suggestions and Annika's estimation of her sister rose another notch. She hoped to gather more details tomorrow, at the cruiser decorating, when Nate was there. The mystery about the blaze switching could possibly be a subject for some future podcast episode, and she figured the sheriff would have some details to use in it.

CHAPTER FIFTEEN

NATE ASSUMED SHELLEY would be at work that Friday morning, because he hadn't heard otherwise. He hoped her family's talk had gone well and they'd been able to make plans that would lead to a good resolution for all of them.

For a large part of Nate's childhood, there'd only been him and his mother until she married Paul Clarkson. He never knew the reason for their breakup and lost all contact with the man.

He and Walter would never have a traditional father-son relationship because Walter had missed Nate's entire childhood and youth. Paul had been the one to take Nate to the occasional baseball game or to come with Nate's mother, Catherine, to school events. Nate had sent a card informing him of his mother's death but never received a reply. Not that it mattered a lot, because other than a few minutes of catching up on the intervening years, what more could people talk about after such a long separation?

The sun was beginning to rise at seven o'clock

and the pink glow in the eastern sky told Nate the day promised to be a nice one. As he passed the Manor, he slowed down to see if there were any lights on at the cottage where Annika was staying. Not yet. Maybe she was a late sleeper, though he recalled that the night he'd crashed on her sofa, she'd already been up and had made breakfast before him.

Of course, he'd had perfectly reasonable excuses for sleeping in that morning. Hours searching the Trail for Stanley, finding him with a bag of money clutched in his hands and getting him transported to hospital. Luckily, Finn had brought his special backpack with the fold-up stretcher, but unluckily for Nate, he'd been the emergency helper. The slog along the Trail had been exhausting—twisting and turning along the path, ensuring Stanley didn't fall off while he'd moaned about his ankle the whole time. Then they'd had to wait for the ambulance to arrive at the entrance to the Trail, outside the Manor. Nate had felt much satisfaction turning Wolchuk over to Bennington Police at the hospital.

Last night, he'd lain awake reflecting on his first week policing in Otter Valley. Despite his initial fear that ticketing illegally parked cars would constitute the bulk of his time, he'd managed to charge Stanley Wolchuk with mischief and now, embezzlement, collaborating with Bennington Police; he'd carried through on a promise of community involvement, and he'd helped a family in crisis—as much as he could, at any rate. Once he'd mentally ticked off those achievements, he came round to the items still on his agenda—Walter and Annika. They had nothing to do with policing, but everything to do with his peace of mind.

The mystery of the blazes had yet to be solved, though, and today Finn intended to take some of his fellow volunteers out on the Trail to correct the signs. The vandalism could have led to more worrying consequences than a flyer on a windshield. Getting lost in a forested area like the Appalachian Trail would be a terrifying experience that Nate, a longtime big-city dweller, didn't even want to imagine.

Shelley hadn't reported for work when Nate arrived at the station, and he debated texting or phoning her to see if everything was okay, but by the time he was trying to figure out her coffee maker, she was walking through the door. She gave him a big smile and set a plastic container on his desk.

"Blueberry muffins," she announced, "and thanks again for your understanding yesterday." Then she noticed Nate fiddling with the coffee maker. "Want me to finish with that?"

"Yes please, Shelley, and thank you for muffins! I didn't get breakfast this morning."

"Oh?"

"I wanted to come in early to finish my report about Stanley Wolchuk and also look for the decorations for the cruiser. People are coming this afternoon to work on it for the parade tomorrow. My plan is to drive it to the community center between four and five, barring any emergency callouts, of course."

Shelley held up two crossed fingers. "There's been enough excitement here already. Far more in a week or so than we had in a month when Sheriff Anderson was in charge."

Nate wasn't sure if that was a compliment or not. He did worry that Chief McNaught might decide to send some reinforcements to the station, which would relegate Nate's position to one of supervision. Desk duty. Nate did not want that.

"What can I help you with right now, then?" Shelley asked as she hung up her coat.

"Could you type up my report? Chief McNaught's old-school and wants a hard copy as well as a PDF file. I left it on your desk and apologize in advance for the handwriting."

"No one knows how to handwrite anymore," Shelley complained. "What else can I do, after typing this report?"

"Could you go and look in the basement for the decorations sometime today?" he asked.

"Sure. What're your plans for the day, before the cruiser decorating happens?" she asked as she switched on the coffee maker.

"I'm checking on Stanley Wolchuk this morning. He was supposed to be transferred to the Bennington police station after he was discharged from the hospital. Then I'm paying his wife a visit."

"But haven't Bennington taken over the case?"

"Yes, but something about it bothers me. I'm not convinced that his wife didn't know anything about his plans."

"You think she was in on it?"

"Maybe. She struck me as a very strong personality, and I doubt much escapes her where Stanley's concerned. I wouldn't be surprised if she was the instigator. Though by now, Stanley might have confessed that to the Bennington officers."

"You have good instincts, Sheriff, for people and what motivates them, I mean."

The compliment was nice, and Nate appreciated her thoughtfulness, but he knew his instincts about one person in his life—Annika—weren't exactly stellar. He figured he'd made some assumptions about her, especially when journalistic principles were involved, that were unfair.

Maybe there'd be an opportunity to amend that after the cruiser decorating. He hoped so, because looking back at the events of the past two days and last night's thoughts about the missed opportunities in his life, he'd come to the conclusion that most mistakes could be forgiven as long as they were acknowledged.

ANNIKA WAS WAITING in line at Tasty Delights Bakery mentally counting the number of cookies she'd need to buy, when she overheard something. The place was busy, even for a Friday afternoon, and most of those behind her were tourists. Or so she assumed, because they definitely weren't residents of Maple Glen. She'd come to buy treats for the cruiser decorating volunteers and for anyone else hanging about the community center, getting ready for tomorrow's parade and Halloween events.

"Did you upload the photos you took on our hike to the website?"

"Of course, but we should have changed the signs back."

A woman, replying to a man's question about uploading photos, but Annika's attention wasn't caught until that comment about the signs. She wanted to turn around but knew that would alert the people speaking quietly behind her. Instead, she sneaked her cell phone out of her coat pocket and pressed Record.

"Even better that we didn't. That was the point, wasn't it? We wanted to change the signs to create confusion for hikers and to rile up the community. Wasn't it intended to attract more readers and get more comments? All that leads to more sponsor money. I still think we should have taken a video."

"We had to be quick. Anyway, I'm going to go back to the B and B after we get food for everyone. I think we should just hang out there until we leave."

"Suit yourself, but I saw flyers for a Halloween parade tomorrow and the place will be hopping. We could go back and do some filming and add it to our site. Halloween is the perfect introduction, right? Think of the 'likes' we'll get."

The talk about changing signs and uploading photos convinced Annika these were the people responsible for switching the blazes on the Trail. She barely heard the somewhat impatient "Yes?" when the person ahead of her walked away and Annika was standing speechless in front of a young man. Her thoughts raced. How many cookies did she need, and who were those people?

"Um, three dozen cookies please."

"What kind? An assortment or…?"

She snapped to attention. "An assortment."

Annika considered her options while the bakery clerk was getting her order. Following those people, or rushing back to the community center where Nate might be? Since she knew where the group was staying, telling Nate was the best plan. When her order was ready, she handed over the money and slowly turned around.

The two people looked to be in their twenties, both with long hair and the man had a small goatee. She didn't dare look longer, as she passed them, but checked them out from behind. Jeans, hoodies, sneakers. Nothing stood out. However, she knew where they were staying.

The community center was buzzing with people when she walked through the main door. A sign informed helpers that refreshments and information could be found in the gym, straight ahead. The decorating was happening outside at the southeast corner of the parking lot.

Annika rushed to one of the tables in the gym where she saw Maura, with her baby snuggled against her in a carry pouch, organizing some teen volunteers.

"Here are the cookies for everyone," Annika said, a bit breathlessly.

"Great. Can you sort out a platter or something for them?" Maura asked as she helped one of the students writing out a sign.

"Uh, in a minute. I really need to find Nate."

Maura turned to look at Annika. "*Nate?*" she teased. "Sheriff Gallagher is out in the parking lot supervising the decorating."

Annika set the box of cookies down and headed for the front door. Some youths were taping orange and black streamers along the sides of the police cruiser in the parking lot while others were sticking on paper jack-o'-lanterns. A large plastic storage container sat at the rear of the vehicle, where Nate stood talking to Leni's husband. Will, Annika remembered.

Nate's smile was casual as she approached, but he didn't stop talking to Will. Annika heard him say something about the farm shop as she reached them, but his smile shifted to a frown when she interrupted him.

"Sorry, but Nate, I have something important you need to hear." She dug into her coat pocket for her phone. "I just came from the bakery where I heard these people talking, and I think they were referring to the blaze switching. Listen." Both men stood close beside her as she pressed Play, with volume at the max.

When it finished, Nate frowned. "Who are these people?"

"They're a group staying at Bernie's."

"And?"

"I think they're the ones who switched the blaze markers on the Trail."

Will pulled his head back in surprise. "Switching blaze markers?" he asked, looking from her to Nate.

Annika saw the rise of color in Nate's neck and knew she'd goofed. She ought to have taken him aside.

Nate recovered well, though. "Some people took the wrong way while hiking the other day. Must have read the markers wrong," he told Will. Then he turned his attention back to Annika.

Will seemed to get the message that Nate wanted to speak to her alone. "Right, okay. See you two at the parade tomorrow." He sauntered toward the front door of the center.

"What's going on, Annika?" Nate asked.

"I think they're the group of paranormal enthusiasts that Bernie told me about my first morning at the B and B."

"And?" He raised his arms in a "so what" gesture.

"They must be the ones who switched the blazes."

"What makes you leap to that conclusion?"

"It's not a leap, Nate. The words speak for themselves. Do you want me to play it again?" She felt hot and tired and frustrated.

"Words out of context can be interpreted in

many ways. This isn't evidence of anything." He paused for a quick second to add, in a gentler tone, "Not everything is a podcast subject."

That stung. "Then I'll get evidence." She swung around to leave, but he placed his hand on her arm.

"Listen, go back to your place. I'll come by when this is finished—" he gestured to the cruiser decorating "—and we'll both listen together and discuss."

"Fine," was all she said. But none of it felt fine to her. He clearly thought she was overreacting or worse, being melodramatic. Maybe a visit back to the B and B on her way to get the evidence he wanted would make her feel better.

CHAPTER SIXTEEN

NATE REGRETTED THE way he and Annika had parted and hoped he'd get a chance to explain his response to the recording she'd made. He'd embarrassed her in front of Will and sensed that part of his response had stemmed from the thought that Will might have concluded Nate and Annika were a couple. Whatever happened between Annika and him, he needed to focus on his job and duty to people in Maple Glen and beyond.

Before driving to the community center so the volunteers could decorate the cruiser, he'd visited Agnes Wolchuk. She already knew the latest about her husband, now awaiting a bail hearing on the embezzlement charges. That wouldn't happen until Monday, so Stanley would remain in a Bennington jail until then. He'd found Agnes to be stoic and reserved, not emotional the way a wife might be on learning her husband could be imprisoned. When she'd asked about the status of the bag of money, wanting to know if it could be redeposited in their bank account, Nate had informed her that the money was in an evidence locker at the Bennington police station where it would remain until the trial. Her reaction had been interesting—the flash of horrified understanding and apparent lack of concern for her husband convinced him his instinct about her had been right. But unless she or Stanley confessed, he had no proof that she was part of the scam.

The case reminded Nate of others he'd encountered in his policing career—people conspiring in criminal acts and then turning on one another when caught. Those cases and others far worse had led to an overwhelming disenchantment with the job. That had taken some time to sink in, and when he'd discovered the corruption amongst his fellow officers, he knew he could no longer stay with the Boston precinct and had searched for police work that was more low-key. He smiled at the irony of those last two words. Thus far, law enforcement in Otter Valley had been anything but low-key. He had yet to decide if that was a good thing or not. What was definitely not such a good thing was the ongoing collision of his personal and professional interests.

From the first day they'd met, when he'd pulled Annika over for speeding on the way to Bennington, he'd been swayed by her captivating smile. He'd had no official status at the time to hand out a ticket or even to stop her in the first place, and his interactions with her continued to lead to situations that bordered on a loosening of rules. The fact that he was attracted to her was a complication.

She was marching off to confront people about the markers on the Trail, even though he'd asked her not to get involved. He had a legitimate reason to go to the B and B and interview them about the blaze switching, and was intending to, but now she'd forced his hand. Depending on her approach, they might decide to leave Maple Glen before he had a chance to talk to them. But he needed to get someone to supervise the rest of the cruiser decorating, which wouldn't take much longer, judging from the waning enthusiasm of the teenagers involved. He found Will Bower chatting to Theo Danby.

"Hey, Will, can you supervise the cruiser decorating? I want to follow up a case I've been working on."

"Oh, the Trail marker thing?"

Nate silently cursed the Glen grapevine. "Uh yeah, think I'll head over to the B and B and see if those people have left."

"Right. What's Annika's interest with them, anyway?"

"She may want to interview them for one of her podcast episodes."

"Okay, and would that be a problem?"

"Switching those markers was vandalism and could lead to a charge. Hikers might have gotten lost or been hurt." He thought of Stanley—so far, the only consequence of the switching. Of course, if the man hadn't fallen, Nate might never have connected him to the embezzlement and the Wolchuks might have gotten away with a crime. But all that was serendipity, Nate figured. Lucky for him, but not for the Wolchuks.

"Right. Let me know if there's anything else I can do for you."

The distance from the community center to the B and B wasn't far, but Nate stopped to send a text to Annika, hoping she'd notice it before he arrived. He kept getting waylaid by people who assumed he knew everything about the weekend events, which added to his anxiety about getting to the Shady Nook at the right moment.

The front door was ajar, and Nate paused on the threshold, wondering if he'd ever be accustomed to that community trust in the innate honesty in people. Maybe when the cynicism he'd acquired in law enforcement could be tempered by living and working in a place like Maple Glen for an extended period. But that was yet to be decided.

He followed a low rumble of conversation along the hall separating the parlor from the dining area into a back room that Nate had never seen. Bernie's own living quarters, he assumed. The room was mostly kitchen where Bernie cooked breakfast for customers, and Nate stood for a second taking in the old-fashioned appliances, wooden counters and shelves of dishes, canned goods and condiments. At the far end was a sitting area, with a small table, one chair and a low settee for two. Annika was sitting in the single chair with her cell phone resting on the table while a young man and woman, both wearing long, patterned robes, were on the settee conversing with her. Nate saw cuffs of jeans and hiking boots protruding from beneath their robes. Fragments of dead leaves clung to the sides and tops of their boots. Evidence of a recent walk on the Trail?

"Afternoon folks," he said, walking toward them. He purposely avoided looking at Annika, fearing her face might give their game away. His interest focused on the couple's reaction to his uniform. The man frowned and sat taller, almost defensively, while the woman looked worried.

"Sorry for the interruption." He glanced meaningfully at Annika who reached for her cell phone and turned it off. "But I have some questions for you two," he said, adding, "although you may leave, Ms. Morrison, and may I please have your cell phone before you go?"

She nodded and without a word, got up, handed him her phone and left the room.

Nate appreciated that, because he didn't want to lose the momentum of this confrontation. He didn't need to listen to Annika's recording for confirmation, because he thought the couple might be the ones responsible for the blaze switching, and he guessed the woman would be the first to admit it.

He sat in the chair Annika had just vacated and set her phone on the table. "Obviously I can't play what Ms. Morrison has recorded without her permission. I intend to get that permission or a warrant to do so, if necessary. But my job will be much easier if you voluntarily answer some questions. What happens afterward will depend on how satisfied I am with your replies." His attention lingered on the woman a moment longer and, as he'd suspected, she was the first to yield.

"I tried to persuade Desmond to switch those signs back to their original positions, but he wanted to keep them like that until we could make our video." Her partner muttered something that Nate interpreted as a warning not to talk.

"Sir," Nate said, raising his voice, "if I have to escort you both to the local station for this interview, I will." He turned back to the woman. "And you are…?"

"Marie." She looked anxiously from Desmond to Nate before continuing. "We belong to a group called The Seekers that searches for evidence of paranormal sightings or signs of possible other-worldly occurrences."

"Okay…" Nate waited patiently.

"We receive donations to our blog and website from people who also believe in the supernatural and who want to support our work. We've accumulated thousands of 'likes' and hundreds of comments on our social media accounts," Desmond added, his voice ringing with pride.

"All of which leads to more money." Nate didn't get it but knew some people could be duped into sending money for almost anything.

"Exactly! That's how we earn our living," Marie exclaimed.

"I can think of less deceptive ways to make money," Nate commented.

Desmond spoke up. "We don't deceive people. If they choose to believe in those things, that's their right. We've done nothing wrong here."

"Until you vandalized government property on government land for purposes of fraud. That's public mischief…maybe more…and I'm here to give you a choice."

Marie was sniffling and Desmond was showing the first signs of unease. Nate figured his options would be accepted. "You will delete all posts on your blog pertaining to Maple Glen and the Appalachian Trail. Next, you are denied access to the Trail and will be arrested if you set foot on any part of it. You can stay in Maple Glen, if that's your preference, or you can leave. Frankly, I suggest you leave." He didn't have to wait long for their answer.

Marie rose from the settee and, glaring at Desmond, swept out of the room. To pack, Nate guessed.

Desmond took a minute longer. When he finally gave up, he announced, "Following those unreasonable demands won't make a difference to our publicity. We've already given an interview to another podcaster who told us it will be aired a day before Halloween, and I assure you that many of our followers will make the trek here to search for supernatural events in your Maple Glen."

Nate watched him march out of the room, holding on to his dignity like some deposed monarch. Ousting the so-called Seekers hadn't been difficult, and he had Annika to thank for playing along.

ANNIKA FIGURED NATE would return her phone after he'd escorted Marie and Desmond out of

Maple Glen. She'd seen from his expression that he was relieved to find her recording the interview with the two paranormal enthusiasts—The Seekers. The name was grandiose, she thought, as if they were searching for some kind of truth when all they really wanted were more fake stories to upload to their website.

After she'd received Nate's text asking her to go along with his plan, she'd promised the couple that she'd use the recording in a podcast episode for her *Folklore and Legends in Small-Town America* series and they were keen to talk. They'd seemed proud of their success cheating people, and Annika hoped if she decided to air a podcast episode on scams connected to folklore and legends, their website would lose a lot of followers, as well as money.

She had Nate to thank for implying that consequences would be applied to her, too, therefore protecting her from any future online trolling from the pair. She'd had enough negative feedback from her last *We Reveal It* episode.

Back at her cottage, she was still exhilarated by her role in the "sting," as Nate had called it, when she heard a quick rap on the front door. He was a bit later than he'd predicted, and she was eager to hear the rest of the story, which he began to recount as soon as he stepped inside.

"They took my advice and left Maple Glen,

under my supervision. I stuck around to make sure they paid Bernie what they owed, and warned them if they returned, they'd go to jail."

"What about all those people who've already been scammed or are about to be? That group needs to be stopped."

"They will be. I've alerted Bennington Police and they're sending the information to Vermont's fraud department. I couldn't have pulled this off without your help, Annika. You were awesomely convincing, especially when you handed over your phone. I hope never to see that facial expression again," he added, grinning. "And thanks for the important prop." He held up her phone and handed it to her. "This is last-minute, but would you like to come and see my decorated police cruiser and check out some of what's currently happening at the community center? Maybe later, head to Wallingford Diner for a bite to eat?"

"I think you already know that I'm a last-minute kind of woman," she quipped.

The stress of getting everything right with Nate's plan was hitting hard and Annika knew diversion was what she needed. "First, something to eat, but how about at my place, for some peace and relaxation, rather than drive to Wallingford?"

"Microwave lasagna, maybe?"

She pretended to think hard. "I do have a nice frozen mac 'n' cheese on hand."

"Hmm, a step up from the lasagna, but I'm thinking a quick trip to the Wallingford Diner to pick up pizzas is a better option."

"Being with you is all I really want," she whispered.

"Likewise," he murmured, pulling her into his arms.

Annika knew two things in that moment: that working with Nate Gallagher had been awesome, and that she was definitely in love with him. She was overcome with the urge to tell him what he meant to her, but the ringtone of his cell phone intervened.

He let go of her to pull his phone out of his jeans pocket. He listened for what seemed ages, until he finally said, "Good to hear. Thanks for letting me know, sir," and turned off his phone.

"You'll be happy to know that The Seekers are in custody in Bennington. Apparently, there's a warrant out for them for fraud in a couple of other states, and Chief McNaught, in Bennington, would like you to send him a copy of your interview with them. He thanked you for your help and reminded me that at some future time you may be required to testify in court." He kept his eyes on her and added, "Until then, he's asking you not to air the interview in a podcast."

Annika had worried that might happen. Perhaps she could convince Walter Ingram to change his mind about being interviewed for the series. If not, then she might have to contact Liz and brainstorm the possibility of resurrecting their *We Reveal It* series about small-town political corruption, if they could find a current and newsworthy candidate. Right now, she was at a complete loss regarding another podcast topic, and her stress was mounting. Bills to pay, a future career at risk of failure.

"Okay, sure. Guess I have no choice."

He shook his head. "Not for the immediate present, but it all depends on whether a decision is made to prosecute them. Then, who knows?"

His shrug told her they'd reached the end of the discussion about The Seekers. A flicker of unease kept her from taking it further. *He's a police officer*, she reminded herself, *and he abides by the law.* What did that bode for any further collaboration with a very law-abiding officer when one person was willing to ignore legal technicalities?

Annika guessed she'd find out sooner than later.

CHAPTER SEVENTEEN

THE DECORATED POLICE cruiser was sitting in a corner of the community center parking lot, with yellow caution tape surrounding it. Two folding chairs had been carried out from the community center and were currently being filled by Finn McAllister and Will Bower. Nate and Annika had walked over together from her place after wolfing down their pizzas, and she went ahead inside, while Nate strolled over to chat with the two men.

"Gents, thanks for standing by. I'm here to relieve one of you, or both for that matter. Has interest in the car been high or…?"

Finn shook his head. "In the beginning, some friends of the kids decorating it came by for some good-natured heckling. Then about half an hour ago, they remembered there was decorating for the teen dance planned for later tonight and took off."

"A teen dance! Don't the adults get one, too?" joked Will.

"You've already attended the best dance of your life, buddy." Finn clapped Will on the shoulder.

Nate figured they'd seen the question in his face, because Finn explained, "Will and his wife, Leni, fell in love at the last big dance here in Maple Glen. St. Valentine's, last year."

"Which was the culmination of a long adolescent crush," Will clarified.

"Let me remind you that everyone else at that dance saw what was happening, except you and Leni," Finn teased. Will's face flushed even more when Finn added, "And it took you a few more weeks to figure that out, too."

"Just playing hard to get," Will said, waving a hand. Then he turned his attention to Nate. "All set for the parade and celebrations tomorrow? People here in the Glen take these events very seriously."

Nate saw his wink. "I think I can handle it. We had community events back in Boston, too, but on a larger scale."

"Boston, eh? What made you apply for the job here in pokey Maple Glen?"

Nate had figured everyone already knew everything about him, thanks to the grapevine. "Burnout," he said.

"I get that. Same thing prompted me to take over my family's maple syrup business, rather than reenlist."

"Army?"

Will nodded but didn't elaborate.

He didn't need to, Nate was thinking. Another high-stress profession. A brief silence fell over the three men, and Nate realized some things don't need to be articulated to be felt or understood.

That was his philosophy about romance, even love. But was that Annika's outlook? How well did he actually know her, beyond superficial interests and pleasures? Even fears? Despite the obvious differences in how they dealt with problems and challenges, they seemed to share the same values, which counted for a lot in any relationship.

He didn't realize someone had asked him a question until a loud throat clearing brought him back to reality. The community center, two relatively new friends.

"About the parade tomorrow," Finn said, "the cruiser is leading the kids' costume parade, along with some local dignitaries, along Church Street to the junction of Route 7, where everyone stops, turns around and goes back to the center for refreshments, games and activities for the kids and the pumpkin carving contest." He must have seen that Nate was struggling to process everything. "I'm sure the Halloween committee, of which you are a member," Finn pointed out, grinning, "has already informed you of the schedule for the whole weekend."

"Uh, sure. It kicks off at ten, right? And everyone assembles at the center about—"

"9:30."

Nate saw that both men looked doubtful about his well-being. "Got it. Just needed confirmation. Okay, next question, who rides with me in the cruiser?"

"Good one," Finn said. "I think Sheriff Anderson always drove it by himself." He looked for acknowledgement to Will, who shrugged and said, "This is my first Halloween parade here in many years."

"How about you, Finn? The fire chief and the sheriff riding together?" Nate asked. Finn hesitated long enough for him to add, "Community teamwork. A good reminder, considering…" He didn't need to finish, as they all remembered the events of the past couple of weeks, when community trust was shaken by the car soaping followed by the parking permit debate.

"Yeah," Finn agreed. "We have a duty to community, don't we Nate, which overrides personal wants and needs? An integral part of our job."

Finn's words stayed with Nate as he went to look for Annika inside the community center. He and Annika had worked well together getting evidence from The Seekers, though he knew she'd hoped to broadcast her interview with the couple. That probably wasn't going to happen, and she'd seemed to accept that fact when he'd gone to talk to her. He was pretty certain he could trust her on that.

The center was swarming with vendors from all over the county setting up tables, people carrying in items for the exhibits of harvest produce and homemade preserves, and kids, taking advantage of parental busyness to run around with abandon. Nate paused a second in the doorway, taking it all in. Organized chaos came to mind, which wasn't his thing at all. Plans, schedules and debriefs had always been part of his character growing up, and even more as an adult.

His mother had smiled when Nate had told her he intended to become a police officer. "The perfect career for you, Nate," she'd said. "You've always liked order in your life, you've always shown empathy for others less fortunate and you've always had a strong sense of justice."

Nate had felt that maternal pride and love throughout his life. Not having a father around had only been an issue a couple of times in his life, as his mother was always there for him. He knew she'd like Annika, and there were times when he wished more than anything that he could introduce Annika to her.

But his stepfather, Paul, was a more complicated matter. He'd only been in Nate's life briefly and they didn't spend a lot of time together. They definitely had nothing resembling a father-son relationship.

None of that mattered anymore, because Nate had now found his biological father. Whether he and Walter Ingram would ever—*could ever*—have a meaningful connection was a question that would eventually be answered. He'd come to Maple Glen to find out more about his actual father, and he'd ended up falling in love with a woman who continued to be a mystery to him. Those were two completely different issues, but he sensed a happy outcome for both rested solely on him.

As he wound around the tables and people, he scanned the gym for Annika but also thought he might see Walter Ingram. The man was a beekeeper who ran a local honey business and surely would have items for sale. Thanks to the internet and local gossip, Nate knew a lot about Ingram except for two missing bits of information—how had Nate's mother and Walter met, and why had their relationship ended. He planned to get answers to both, soon.

Halfway around the gym he spotted a familiar figure ahead, red hair brushing her shoulders, straight-backed and wearing jeans and a checked flannel shirt that appeared to have straps attached to it. Had to be Annika, but there was something about the way she was standing that made him pause. He'd almost reached her when she swung around, and the unusual strapping was immediately explained.

A small downy head peeped up from the baby carrier that she was wearing. Nate immediately realized two things—Annika looked perfectly at ease in her new role and the smile she was bestowing on the baby shone with a contentment that Nate had never seen in her. He took a moment for this picture to set permanently in his mind, because he thought it would give him a happy memory to look back on no matter what the future held for him.

ANNIKA STOOD AGAINST the wall at one end of the community center gym surveying the flashing light of a disco ball that some elderly Glen resident unearthed from a large locker in the center's basement. "Can't believe it!" he'd exclaimed, "It's been years since I last saw this."

Annika could believe it, as she checked out the cobwebs and a few missing pieces of mirrored facets. Many years, she decided. Yet Finn had appeared with a tall ladder, which he easily climbed thanks to years of firefighting, while Will and a couple of other men held the ladder steady, and soon the ball was strobing many colorful lights, if a bit spotty in places.

She'd counted approximately twenty teens and preteens in line outside the center's main door when she'd arrived for chaperone duty twenty minutes before the dance was scheduled to start at 7:30 p.m. Flyers about Maple Glen's Halloween weekend had been distributed in Wallingford as well, so event organizers knew there'd be more adolescents attending than the few in Maple Glen. Devon had told her that Finn and some of his colleagues had surveyed the area of the gym and its exit doors a week or so ago and decided to limit the number of attendees to fifty, which had been printed on the flyers. Annika, recalling her own teen experiences, was worried that more might show up, but she knew Nate would be arriving shortly to assist.

The memory of his expression when he'd found her helping out earlier was still vivid enough that she found herself drifting back to the tenderness in his eyes and his smile, which was a combination of surprise and pleasure. But what had astonished her most of all, was the contentment she'd felt with Maura's baby tucked against her. That special baby scent she'd heard people refer to was a real thing, she'd found, and the warmth of his body filled her with a sensation she'd never experienced—the instinctive urge to protect him, to place a hand against his back and head when she bent down, despite knowing the carrier had all the necessary safeguards. The most interesting thing of all, Annika felt, was that as an adult she'd never considered motherhood an option. Building a career had always been her sole focus.

When Maura had asked her to wear the carrier with a sleeping Colin tucked inside while she and her volunteers made up signs for the donkey riding in the field adjacent to the community center parking lot, Annika's first thought had been, why me? Surely there were more adept women here—mothers and grandmothers—that would be a better choice. That was reinforced when people started coming up to her to coo over the baby and to ask questions—how old is he, is he sleeping through the night or is he teething? Her inability to answer highlighted incompetence as a mother, which brought occasional frowns from those who didn't know her. Her friends in the Glen had merely grinned, while Devon had teased, "Looks good on you, sister."

The amazing thing was, by the time Maura returned to collect what she called her "precious package," Annika had become so accustomed to Colin's heft and warmth that she'd felt an overwhelming nakedness when Maura unstrapped and removed the carrier, with Colin still fast asleep inside it. She was jarred out of that memory at a sudden tap on her shoulder and, as she wheeled around, saw Nate at her side.

"Does this bring back memories for you?" he asked, gesturing to the dance floor where some of the teens were now mingling, though not actually dancing.

"Totally! And for you?"

"Kind of. I went to an all-male boarding school for a few years, when I was about eleven."

"Oh? Was that a good thing or not?"

"Not in the beginning, but fortunately for me it was actually a great school, though with a slight leaning toward the military. I ended up liking it, but left when I was fifteen so…" He shrugged without elaborating.

Annika was surprised at the revelation and would have asked more questions, but his expression shut down that thought immediately. She realized there was a lot more to learn about Nate Gallagher, and she hoped she'd have the chance to discover all of it before she had to leave Maple Glen. That day would inevitably come once her contract with Venture was completed.

The last dance of the evening was announced by one of the teen organizers, Luke Danby, who commented at some good-natured booing, "Make sure you're on the committee for the next dance. We can always use more volunteers." He gave a thumbs-up to the DJ the committee had hired and silence fell over the gym as a much-loved slow song played.

Annika looked at Nate and smiled.

"Shall we?" he asked.

"Why not?" She slipped her hand into his and he led her onto the dance floor.

He wrapped his arms around her, gently pulling her close enough that she could feel the beat of his heart beneath his sweater. They moved together as if they'd been dance partners their whole lives and Annika wished the music, and the night, would never end.

CHAPTER EIGHTEEN

NATE SLEPT THROUGH his cell phone alarm the morning after the teen dance. Today was the Halloween parade and he had to be at the community center by 9:30 at the latest. He couldn't even blame his sleeping in on a late night, because he and Annika had parted shortly after the dance ended at ten o'clock. Her agenda for the next day included helping the youngsters get into their costumes for the parade, as well as working with other volunteers to set up the gym for the day's activities, both inside and out. But they'd had to hang around after the dance supervising cleanup, and Nate continued to be impressed by the small group of adolescent volunteers—Luke Danby, Ashley Watson—related to Bernie, he'd learned—Will's stepson, Max, and a few other teens from the area—who stayed late as well.

The kids were a tight group due to the small size of Maple Glen and surprisingly, age differences didn't affect that solidarity. Nate thought back to his own adolescence at boarding school and later, growing up in Boston and wondered if he'd be the same person he was now had those former friendships been more lasting.

He thought about Finn, who'd been raised in Maple Glen and was now settled here with the love of his life. Will had left but returned to his roots to take over a family business. Nate was the lone newcomer in their group, and he had a feeling that tag would stick with him for a while if he settled into village life.

He made coffee while he showered, poured it into a thermos and grabbed a granola bar on his way out the door. The thermos reminded him of the night of the stakeout, when Annika had awakened him with much-needed caffeine. Was that when friendship began to change for them, shifting to something deeper while they chatted under the comfort of darkness? So much had happened since that night that Nate questioned whether he'd be able to get back on track with his plan of connecting with his biological father. He hadn't envisioned what might come after, but falling in love had definitely not been on his agenda.

He got to the community center on the dot and saw that many volunteers—including his two new best friends—were already there, chatting, sipping coffee from their own thermoses while shooing youngsters away from the cruiser. He expected some ribbing and wondered how much of Maple Glen had witnessed his slow dance with Annika last night. Probably a good part of the population, and he bet the grapevine had been buzzing. But he was happily surprised at the lack of any teasing from Will and Finn, and it occurred to him as the day went on, that good friends instinctively knew when to rein in those responses. What surprised him was his lack of concern about the public attention, especially considering his worry when he'd first arrived in the Glen about keeping his private life under wraps and separate from work.

While Nate was helping Will and Finn remove the yellow caution tape from around the cruiser, a small school bus pulled into the parking lot and disgorged a group of high schoolers wearing matching uniforms and carrying a variety of musical instruments.

"How big is this parade going to be?" Nate asked, watching the teens rallying outside the bus.

"Small for cities, but big for here," Finn said.

"Will it kick off exactly at 10:00?"

"One can only hope," Finn said, grinning.

Nate spotted Luke and Ashley in the band group and guessed they were involved in a lot of community events. A great outlet for all that adolescent energy and insecurity, and he thought he should ask Shelley Barnett if her son, Jason, was part of the Youth Club group or maybe interested in joining if the teens were going to be living with her in Wallingford. Either way, he knew he'd have to keep tabs on the teen for a while to make sure he didn't reoffend. Pranks were okay as long as they were harmless to both people and property.

"What was it like for you as a teenager, growing up in Maple Glen?" he asked Finn.

Finn's loud sigh told part of the story. "Limiting," he said. "As my dad used to say, 'everyone knows everything about everybody in Maple Glen.'"

"I might have already heard that expression." Nate grinned.

"Probably, it's become part of the lore of Maple Glen."

"I guess a lot of teens escaped to bigger places as soon as they could."

"I did, and so did Will Bower. My sister, too."

"You have a sister?" Nate was realizing he had much more to learn about the Glen people. Too preoccupied with one resident in particular—Walter Ingram.

"Roxanne, and she has a daughter—my niece, Kaya. I'm hoping they'll both come this weekend."

"I didn't know that," Nate said.

"Well, you haven't been here long, and the old

grapevine is bound to fill you in on most of us sooner or later."

Finn was only half joking, but the comment was a good reminder that not much escaped the vine. Nate thought of Walter again and wondered where he fit on the gossip scale. Near the top, he figured, considering his role in finding the Morrison kids. Nate also wondered what the impact of his own revelation would be on Walter. The Glen grapevine would most certainly spread the word about both of them, speculation feeding its tendrils. Who else would be affected? Devon Fairchild, of course, as that long-ago case would be revived. Perhaps Amelia Owens, who might wish Walter had had enough trust in her to confide his past. Nate wasn't liking those images, and for the first time questioned his decision to confront Walter. It was one thing to expose himself to local gossip, but was it right to resurrect all those other memories for some people in Maple Glen? That might have been the result if Annika had written Walter's story for her podcast.

Fortunately for Nate, all conflicting thoughts about Walter Ingram were put on hold as the parade participants lined up.

Finn gestured to the cruiser and exclaimed, "Let's go!"

Will Bower had spontaneously taken on the

role of parade marshal and was directing adults and kids. Nate saw the man's army training, a reminder that there were instincts, as well as experiences, that stayed with a person throughout one's life. He could live with that knowledge about himself, but could Annika? He sighed as he climbed into the cruiser. *Save that for another day, Gallagher.*

When Finn closed the passenger door, he gave a thumbs-up to Nate, who switched on the cruiser's ignition. At Will's signal from the end of the center's driveway, Nate rolled the cruiser onto Church Street, made a right turn and shifted into Park. He noticed that Will was holding what looked like a walkie-talkie—old technology that still had occasional use—and he wondered who was on the receiving end.

"When I get to the junction of Route 7, I assume the plan is to—"

"Shift into Park again and wait for the entire parade to catch up to you, then Will and Annika are going to marshal everyone in an about-face and head back to the community center. Obviously, we can't enter the highway."

Maybe Annika on the other walkie-talkie, then? "Is someone going to be filming this?" Nate suddenly thought to ask.

"Will's wife, Leni, and my buddy, Matt, from the fire hall."

"What will they do with the footage?" Nate was thinking of Chief McNaught in Bennington and his potential reaction to the cruiser's use. On the other hand, Sheriff Anderson had told him the decorated cruiser was a long-standing tradition in the valley's parade.

"There's a Maple Glen website, though I think the volunteer who updated it grew tired of the task a while ago." Finn paused, adding, "Seems like we might need to get a new custodian for that."

"Don't look at me!" Nate grinned. "But Annika's a writer, you know."

"Uh-oh, I promise not to divulge my source for that suggestion."

Nate laughed. "We must be changing roles here, McAllister." He peered into the outside rearview mirror and saw Will making a "start" gesture with his arm. Then he shifted into Drive and led the costumed children, local dignitaries and some parents along Church Street. Halfway to the turnaround at the junction of Route 7, he spotted a man holding up a young boy on his shoulders for a better vantage point and when Nate waved to them, the youngster's enthusiastic response touched him. He smiled at the boy's exhilaration and for a second wondered what it felt like for a son and father to be celebrating something special. Perhaps, if he were lucky, he might find out some day.

ANNIKA WAS EXHAUSTED and the day had barely begun. The parade participants were trickling in, with the younger children clamoring to get into the activities while parents tried to establish some kind of order, which Annika figured was an impossible task. Her helpers were a mix of teens from the Youth Club and their parents supervising the various indoor activities—the face painting, the art table with its array of crayons and markers, Halloween-themed cookie decorating, thanks to baker Sue Giordano—and the outdoor pumpkin carving, apple bobbing and in the field on the far side of the center, the fake corn maze obstacle course that Max Costa and Luke Danby had created using papier-mâché stalks that were tall enough to challenge a child, but not a teen. The school bus that had been hired to transport the marching band drove kids and parents to Jake & Friends, where Maura Danby and helpers had created a haunted barn. Annika thought the donkeys, braying in the adjacent field, provided the perfect sound effects.

When the parade had backtracked to the community center, she'd spotted Nate parking the cruiser in its original place but hadn't seen him since.

Last night he'd walked her to her cottage after the dance, hands clasped together, and had held her in his arms for a long moment at her door.

"Tonight was fun," he'd said, "and I think the kids enjoyed the dance as much as we did."

"I hope they did, though personally, most of the dances I attended as a teenager were either big disappointments or horrible embarrassments."

"Same here. But I think the kids in Maple Glen have an advantage we didn't have."

"What do you mean?"

"They grew up together and…well…they're part of a big, extended family, in a way."

"A community family, you mean?"

"Exactly, and that's a perfect name for it."

Then he'd kissed her on the cheek, murmured "sleep tight" and walked home. Annika had wanted more than anything to call him back, but instead, listened to the calmer voice deep inside, reminding her that some longings were best left unfulfilled. She'd planned to leave Maple Glen once her podcast was completed, returning for Devon's wedding at Thanksgiving, only a month away. Now she was sabotaging those plans by falling in love with a man who was clearly destined to stay.

That was her conclusion after she'd witnessed the admiration and respect for him from all the residents. He'd established a presence in the village and although the continuation of his job depended on an election in one year's time, she knew he'd already won the approval of the residents. The problem was, would the people of Maple Glen accept her, too, once her podcast on local legends was aired?

"This is hardly the place for introspective meditation, or whatever you're doing."

Annika wheeled about to see Devon standing next to her, a teasing smile lighting up her face. "Wondering when the day will end," she admitted.

"Good luck with that. Wanting time to fly doesn't make it happen. Best simply to jump in and get busy."

"Spoken like a true older sister."

"You better believe it!" Devon waited a minute to add, "Seriously though, is everything okay?" Then at Annika's frown, explained, "With you and Nate."

"Sure," Annika mumbled. The community center gym was no place for confidential revelations, and she felt a slight annoyance that her sister had raised the issue.

"Okay, just letting you know I'm always available for a sisterly chat."

"Thanks, Devon, but…um… I'm a bit confused and in the process of working things out. Mentally, I mean."

"Some feelings are best left to enjoy, rather than worry over."

"I suppose, though we don't live in isolation from our thoughts and feelings, do we? There's always the outside world, looming." Annika tried to make light of her serious tone.

"Of course, and we can't ignore it, but take one day at a time, Annika."

"Enjoy the present?" Annika managed a quick smile.

"As the ancient philosophers advised, and as your big sister does, too." Devon patted her on the arm. "The day isn't over yet." She leaned closer and whispered, "Last I saw of him, he was being corralled by Betty Watson to judge the pumpkin carving, and I bet he'd appreciate either some help with that, or an escape from it."

Annika laughed. "Poor Nate, he really can't say no."

"That's why people here like him so much."

Annika frowned. "Because he's a pushover?"

"Oh, he's no pushover," Devon said, shaking her head for emphasis. "He's always ready to listen, patiently and quietly. He doesn't rush to judgment. He's willing to give second chances to people who need them."

She was right, Annika thought. Nate was simply a good person, who happened to be a police officer, who happened to be the man she loved. He set a high benchmark, and she hoped she could meet it.

"Thanks, sis, for words of wisdom." She hugged Devon, grateful for the auspicious discovery of a letter that had brought them together.

CHAPTER NINETEEN

IT WAS JUST past noon, and Nate was ready to call it a day. As much as he'd enjoyed the bustle and the almost frenetic energy in the center, he needed some alone time to contemplate next steps with Annika, but even more, to decide how and when he'd confront Walter Ingram. Before the parade, when he'd been talking to Finn about growing up in Maple Glen, he'd found himself doubting the wisdom of revealing himself to Walter, but he'd read his mother's letter so many times it was etched in his memory, and it surfaced again as a timely reminder.

> Please forgive me if this information causes you problems. I simply wanted you to make the decision to contact Walter when you were an adult. You've been the best son a mother could possibly want, and I wish you happiness and true love in your life, wherever you find it.

Obviously, that one-on-one meeting wasn't going to happen at the community center, in full view of the eyes of Maple Glen, but he decided to make some excuse to visit Walter at his home, later in the day. Even tomorrow, Nate thought, and scolded himself for procrastinating again. He wound his way through the gym until he found Ingram's display at the end of the furthest row of tables. Walter wasn't there, but Amelia Owens was.

"Sheriff Gallagher," she announced with a big smile. "Are you enjoying the festivities or champing at the bit to get back home?"

"A little bit of both," Nate admitted. "How about you?"

"Same here. I'm at an age when a little excitement quickly becomes too much excitement."

"I know exactly what you mean." He hesitated, trying to come up with a plausible excuse for looking for Walter, but Amelia solved that problem.

"The day has been exhausting for Walter, so I sent him home. His new hip is still giving him some grief and, like me, he's no spring chicken."

"I doubt age has slowed you down, Amelia."

"Aw, I knew there was a reason I liked you." She patted his arm. "Pull up his chair and talk to me." She pointed to the one next to her.

He sat down and took a minute to survey the

display of jars of honey, their labels identifying seasons and flowers: Clover, early spring. Apple trees, late spring. Basswood trees, early summer. Milkweed, midsummer. New England Aster, late summer, early fall.

A whole year taken care of, except, of course, for winter. Nate was curious. What exactly did bees do in the long, Vermont winters? He voiced the question to Amelia.

"Walter could explain it much better than I. They hunker down in the hive, I think, and wait it out." She paused to add, "I expect he'll be back after a nap. Why don't you return in an hour or so?"

"Sure." Nate knew this was his chance to get information about Walter from someone who'd known him for many years, though how to achieve that without sounding like an interrogator?

"You and Walter have had a long friendship, I guess. Since he found the Morrisons on the Long Trail," he began.

"Chloe and Billy." Amelia seemed to drift back in time for a moment. "Everything changed for so many of us from that very day."

"Well, definitely for Chloe and Billy—or Devon and Dan, as they later became. But how was it for you, and…uh… Walter?"

"For me, I continued working for the Department for Children and Families until I took early retirement a year or so ago. I'm a bit younger than Walter," she said, smiling, "but we worked so closely together those few days that we got to know each very well, and discovered, through subsequent emails and phone calls, that we had a lot in common." She fell silent for a long moment. "Walter was legally separated from his wife at the time, and our friendship eventually grew into something deeper. But we both valued—and still do—our independent lifestyles and decided to continue in a kind of long-distance relationship."

Nate immediately thought of Annika and their inevitable separation. "How did that work? Did you find the distance a positive or negative influence on your feelings for one another?"

"Hmm, a combination of both, I think. We began as acquaintances, then went on to friendship and…well…" Her face turned red. "I think you're old enough to put the rest of the equation together, Nate."

"Do you know anything about his wife, why they separated?" Nate was certain that wife hadn't been his mother but wanted to rule the possibility out.

"Not much." She heaved a sigh. "In many ways, Walter is a very private person. Information about his past may be revealed occasionally through some connecting memory, but that's it.

I do know he took early retirement from the fire department following a horrific traffic accident near here years ago and he never got over the trauma of helping those involved. I think the nonstop media frenzy when he found the Morrison kids, followed by the accident just naturally pushed him into retirement."

"And his wife?"

"They were already separated by the time he found Chloe and Billy and divorced afterwards."

"Did he have a previous wife, before the divorced one, I mean?"

Amelia frowned. "What's with all these questions, Nate Gallagher? You really need to be asking Walter." Then she added, "Are you working with Annika on a podcast about him? Because you know Walter wouldn't be happy about that."

This would be the perfect time to confide in Amelia—a woman who appeared to have a gift for inviting confidences—but he held back. The moment would come soon enough, and it would happen only with Walter.

"No, no. Just that…um… I have a relative who read about all this in the papers and was curious." Nate hoped he wasn't blushing from the white lie, though his mother had been a very close relative. He wished more than ever that she'd told him the truth years ago, rather than leaving him a letter.

"Hmm," was her comment.

Nate was aware of her keen appraisal of him, and as someone who seldom prevaricated, much less actually lied, he knew he wasn't a good enough actor to continue. He let enough time pass to reduce any further suspicion about his questions, and finally asked, "Which honey do you recommend?" He tilted his head to the jars on the table.

The subterfuge didn't fool her at all. "I think you ought to talk to Walter about his past if it's important to you. And meanwhile, where's that lovely young friend of yours? Annika?"

Where indeed, Nate was thinking. "Helping out somewhere in here, I guess."

"Have you been a couple long?"

"Uh, we're not exactly what one might call a 'couple,'" he said, realizing the tables were turned now. He couldn't quite interpret Amelia's smile, but he knew she'd never be duped by scammers like The Seekers.

"Walter and I don't know her very well yet, but her status as Devon's half-sister raises her quite a notch in our estimation and, I imagine, also in the minds of Maple Glen residents."

Nate completely agreed with her but wasn't certain of her implication. Was she warning him not to hurt Annika, or hinting they ought to make their relationship a more official one?

Or perhaps he was simply misreading her intent. Sometimes verbal cues eluded him, as he tended to draw conclusions about people from their mannerisms and facial expressions. That skill was definitely an asset in police work, but not so much in a love relationship when assumptions could be dangerously misleading.

There were good reasons why Nate questioned proclamations of love. His mother must surely have heard them from Walter Ingram, his biological father, and later, from Paul Clarkson, his stepfather for a brief period. Two men who subsequently abandoned his mother, leaving her with a child to raise on her own.

Nate knew he could never do that, no matter what the cost. All the more reason to keep his feelings for Annika in check. The notion brought a smile. *A bit late for that, Gallagher.*

ANNIKA WAS FAMISHED. There were a couple of food trucks from Wallingford set up at the far end of the parking lot, with long lineups, and Leni's farm shop was closed due to the ongoing Halloween festivities. Her options were limited to a drive to the Wallingford Diner or lunch at home. Cheese and crackers, or scrambled eggs and toast? She wondered which would appeal to Nate and decided to look for him to find out, though food wasn't the only thing on her mind.

Last night's kiss at her doorstep hadn't been a blissful end to a memorable evening. It ought to have been, in a perfect world of romance and love, but instead it had led to more questions than answers. One part of her wanted promises and commitments, while the other, more realistic side, reminded her she had a podcast deadline and an eventual return to New Hampshire. Her stay in Maple Glen had always been temporary, and she'd forgotten that.

As much as they were aligned in values and attitudes, she felt that she and Nate sometimes had opposing perspectives due to their different backgrounds. Not that she knew a lot about his upbringing because he never talked about his parents or his childhood, and she too, had kept much of her life private. What kind of future could they have as partners if they didn't share their pasts?

Too many questions on an empty stomach, Annika decided. She was on her second round of the community center gym when she spotted Nate walking away from Amelia Owens at Walter Ingram's display of honey. He seemed to be on a mission, striding toward the front door of the gym, his face grim with determination, similar to his expression when he'd ordered The Seekers to leave Maple Glen after listening to their bragging confession that she'd recorded.

She was tempted to follow him, but something held her back. Intuition? Or perhaps the sense that he wouldn't appreciate questions about his actions, and as a journalist, Annika would always have something to ask.

She considered approaching Amelia to find out what they might have been discussing but decided the woman wouldn't break a confidence. The best option was to suggest to Nate that they have lunch together. A full stomach guaranteed a relaxed mind, something he might appreciate as a man who likely had more stress in his life than other people due to his job. It could also be a chance to find out what their next steps might be as a couple in Maple Glen.

On her way to locate Nate, she received two texts: the first, from Maura Danby, inviting her to brunch the next day and the second, from Liz, her former business partner and good friend. The latter was the one that stopped her to read it one more time and came as a reminder of her other life outside of Maple Glen.

Hey there! I've been doing some research for a possible new We Reveal It, and found a good one, kind of in your area. A politician in New Hampshire is being investigated for accepting bribes re land development. Check him out on the links below. Paul Clarkson.

There was a vacant chair near the front door and Annika sat down to browse the pertinent links and social media sites with posts about a local scandal in New Hampshire. She texted a thank-you to Liz, adding that she'd get on to it right away.

All thoughts of filling an empty stomach vanished as the familiar hunger for a good story took over. Her bank account was shrinking, and the tip from Liz was timely. She'd lost her focus and needed to get back on track with her podcast plans. Worrying about her chances with Nate Gallagher was distracting her from her goal of a successful career in podcasting, one that would probably take her away from Maple Glen. She'd never intended to stay in the village anyway, so leaving it wouldn't be a wrench. But she felt an unexpected pang of regret that following her career path would most likely mean leaving the sheriff behind.

CHAPTER TWENTY

AS SOON AS Will parked his pickup at the end of the long driveway leading up to the barn behind Maura and Theo Danby's home, Nate had a feeling that the invite to brunch the day after the Halloween celebration was going to involve something more than sitting at a table to eat. This suspicion was confirmed when Maura emerged from the back door of the house, her baby boy strapped against her chest and a smile that was half apologetic and relieved.

"Hello, you two! Thanks so much for coming to my rescue," she said as Nate and Will climbed out of the truck. "And before you leap to any conclusions, I truly believed Theo was going to be home to handle this, but he got called to the clinic for some emergency. Leaving me with a baby and three donkeys that need to be brought into the barn. They don't like rain."

Nate was a tad confused when she pointed skyward until he noticed for the first time a dark and threatening cloudbank looming over the valley. Then he looked toward the field adjacent to the barn and saw three stocky shapes at the far end of it. Donkeys.

He was now wishing he hadn't received Maura's text message, or that she'd been a bit more forthright with her invite so he could have had a plausible excuse. Or escape, he thought. He sneaked a glance at Will to assess the potential danger level of their task, but the man appeared nonplussed by the unexpected request. Annoyingly so, Nate thought.

City people usually had little interaction with large animals, especially four-legged ones. The exception was big dogs, a trend Nate also didn't understand. Why share an apartment with a Great Dane? He simply didn't get it. His childhood pet had been a hamster, and even that furry bundle eventually lost some of its charm after a few months when Nate's mother handed over cage cleaning to Nate.

"Um… I don't know much about donkeys." He looked to Will for support, and finding none, went on to say, "How about Finn? Maybe he could help?"

"I tried him first, but he's on duty today," she said with a sigh. "All you two have to do is go behind them at a distance, of course, raise your arms and shoo them to the barn door. When they go inside, close the door behind them." She shrugged. "Simple."

Hah, easy for you to say, Nate thought. When he glanced at Will again, he saw him nodding. Nate took a calming breath. "Okay," he mumbled, and was about to head for the gate leading into the pasture when he thought of something else. "Anything we should know about them?" He'd spotted one that was much larger than the others. She took a minute to answer, which hiked Nate's stress level.

"The big guy is Roger, and he has a blind eye, on his right side. Shep, his companion dog, is out in the field somewhere and will probably come running when you start shooing them in. He's very friendly and may even help chase them." She laughed. "He's a sheep dog, so the instinct is to herd, even though they're donkeys. And not sheep."

Nate thought her giggle stemmed from nervousness, which added to his own. What wasn't she telling them? The reveal came as soon as he and Will stepped into the field and closed the gate behind them.

"Oh, and keep an eye on Jake," Will said. "The second-largest one. He tends to nip when he's upset."

Nip, as in bite? Nate hung back, letting Will take the lead. He couldn't help thinking that facing down a criminal in Boston had certainly raised stress levels, but his training had taught him to handle that. Whereas he'd had no training at all in managing donkeys and knew virtually nothing about them. Except that now he'd learned they could bite.

Will paused mid-step to look back at him. *Checking to see if I was still following him*, Nate wondered?

"I think the smallest one is Matilda," Will told him. "And I've heard she's very gentle. How about if I corral Jake and you take Matilda? Roger will probably just follow along, with the help of the dog."

"This your first experience with them?" Nate was curious. He knew the stables had been open for public riding but wasn't sure that was still happening.

"Yep. Leni tried to persuade me to go riding with her and the kids once, but I couldn't picture myself on the back of a donkey. Legs hanging almost to the ground." He shook his head. "Nah. Not for me."

"Likewise," Nate said. They were almost halfway when a crack of thunder split the air.

"Uh-oh," muttered Will. "Best get moving."

Nate sped up, propelled by what looked like an impending storm. "What'll happen if…you know…the rain comes before we get them in the barn?"

"Dunno," Will tossed back to Nate. "But we're going to find out real soon."

Nate felt a whoosh of relief when they reached Matilda first. She was chest high and despite her whinny as Nate drew closer, she let him grab her reins. Without biting. Right. *You can do this*, he told himself.

Will headed for Jake and Nate felt a tug of guilt that grew quickly when he noticed his friend stop in front of the donkey. Nate couldn't figure out what Will was doing, because his back was to him. Then the first drops of rain came, and Matilda made some kind of throaty sound that Nate guessed would ramp up in volume if he didn't get her into the barn right away. He cast one last glance over his shoulder as he led Matilda into the barn. He had no idea what to do with her at that point, because Maura's instructions, as far as Nate was concerned, had been cursory…*raise your arms and shoo them towards the barn door.*

But his question was answered almost immediately as Matilda shook her head, causing him to drop her reins, and she trotted down the center aisle toward a stall at the end. A stall that fortunately was open. Nate trotted after her and closed the stall door. One down, two to go.

But just as he reached the barn door, Roger appeared, filling the entire open space. Nate stumbled back from the unexpected billow of hot air exhaling from Roger's nostrils but managed to stop himself from falling. The dog—Shep?—sniffed at Nate's jeans before following Roger to a stall midway along where he waited patiently until Nate thought to shut the stall door.

Now there was only Jake—the biter—somewhere outside with Will. A thought occurred to Nate—and he recalled it with some guilt later that day—that if he waited inside long enough, Will would probably get Jake inside the barn all on his own. But Nate also knew he wouldn't forgive himself if Jake were to bite Will. He took another calming breath and exited the barn, only to quickly step back inside at an ear-splitting bray from Jake.

Will was grinning, but Nate saw his tight grip on the reins. He waited in the barn doorway as Will led Jake to a stall and closed the door, checking to ensure it was locked.

"I think we've done our good deeds for the day, don't you?" Will quipped as he walked toward Nate.

"For sure. Say, it looked like you were talking to Jake. Like some kind of donkey whisperer."

When Will stopped laughing, he admitted,

"Yeah, I told him if he didn't come inside nicely, he might get sent to the glue factory."

"What?"

"When you were a kid, didn't you ever hear an adult refer to old horses going to a glue factory?"

"Uh, nope. I grew up in Boston where I think there might have been horses somewhere, but none I ever encountered as a kid."

"Huh! Anyway, it was all nonsense of course. Like stories about ghosts and goblins at Halloween."

That reminded Nate he had to return the cruiser from the community center to the police station. But then he realized he could drive it there himself tomorrow, his next workday, which was a better option. He could park the cruiser out of sight, behind his house. But if the farm shop had reopened, there'd be traffic passing by the house and if some mischief maker eyed it that could be a problem. An alternative was to move it closer to Annika's place, farther away. That way, he'd have an excuse to see Annika. Not that he needed one anymore. Weren't they now a couple, as Amelia Owens had suggested?

The rain came just as they left the barn, and they dashed for the back door of the farmhouse.

ANNIKA WAS SITTING at one end of Maura's kitchen table when she heard the door of the mudroom crashing open, followed by stomping and thudding noises. She caught Maura's eye and shrugged.

"The men, running from a bit of rain," Maura said.

More like sheets of rain, Annika thought, peering out the window near her chair. A crack of thunder made her jump and baby Colin must have heard it, too, because he stirred inside the snuggly attached to Maura and made a faint mewing sound.

"Uh-oh," Maura whispered. "Just when I need to finish the brunch. And of course, no Theo to help."

"I can help," Annika said. "Just tell me what to do."

"Wear my baby for me for a few minutes?"

"Um, how about handing him to me and I'll rock him a bit?"

"That'll do. Only long enough to finish my frittata and get the bacon going. Thanks!" She unzipped the snuggly and carefully pulled baby Colin out. "Can you grab that blankie there, on the chair next to you?"

"Blankie?" Annika grinned.

"What happens when there's a baby in the house. All words become diminutives. Even Theo is doing it now." She took the small blanket from Annika, wrapped it around Colin and handed him over to her.

He was a little package of warmth that Annika nestled against her, inhaling a mysterious baby scent of talcum and shampoo that wafted up from him. "Do all babies smell like this? Kind of sweet?"

Maura laughed. "They do…until they don't."

Annika caught her meaning. So far, so good she thought. Then the door leading to the mudroom creaked open and Nate strode in, followed by Will Bower. Their faces were streaked with rain, and they were laughing at some joke until they spotted Annika holding a sleeping baby and fell silent.

Maura left the room and returned with two towels which she handed to them, wordlessly pointing to the mudroom. They got her message, retreated quietly and closed the door behind them. "I've got Theo trained not to charge into a room," she said, "but I'm still working on Luke, who's got all the energy of a teenager and is still getting used to life with a baby brother."

"I bet he's an awesome big brother."

"He will be for sure, though right now he's adjusting…like the rest of us." Maura opened the oven door to pull out a tray of crispy bacon and a large cast-iron frying pan holding what looked like an omelet.

Annika's stomach rumbled.

"Was that you or Colin?" Maura asked.

They were still giggling when the men returned, tiptoeing into the kitchen this time. Annika thought the whole scene was like a pantomime, everyone gesturing, nodding or shaking heads while Maura set the brunch onto the table. Then she came over to Annika and held out her arms for Colin.

Although she'd enjoyed the bundle of goodness in her arms, Annika felt a whoosh of relief. When she handed over Colin, she relaxed into her chair and thought perhaps if she were to stay in Maple Glen she could offer to babysit when he was a bit older. The idea startled her because she'd never had much experience with children, let alone babies, and didn't consider herself maternal in any way. Yet how to explain a feeling that was both strange and familiar at the same time?

She glanced across the table and caught Nate staring at her. He flashed a quick smile that reminded Annika of the moment he'd come up to her during the Halloween events at the community center and had seen Colin in the snuggly strapped against her. There'd been more surprise in his smile that day, but the expression of pleasure was the same. As if she'd passed some kind of test. At least, she liked to think she'd passed, but there were sobering moments when the reality of her future days in Maple Glen arose to remind her everything she was experiencing then and there would soon be in the past. Along with Maple Glen itself. The boisterous arrival of the rest of the brunch guests was a welcome relief from those dark thoughts.

Leni Bower, followed by her two children whose names Annika couldn't remember, carried a large flat box of pastries into the kitchen. "Where do you want these, Maura?" She turned and noticed Annika. "Hi, stranger! I haven't seen you in ages."

"On the dining room table, please. It's going to be buffet style, and I think adults and kids can sit wherever they like," Maura said.

"Yay!" shouted the boy, which brought smiles from the adults.

"Okay, Max, you are now the official door greeter," his mother said. "Your job is to tell everyone where to set their offerings of food, and Emma," she turned to smile at the young girl, "your job is to keep an eye on Max, who might be tempted to sample something before it's time."

"For Pete's sake, Mom," Max groaned.

Leni handed him the box, and he headed out of the kitchen and down the hall, followed by his sister.

Annika was impressed by Leni's unflappable management of her children. Was it something that grew slowly, from the day children were born, or more innate, specific to certain types of mothers? Or fathers, for that matter. She glanced at Nate, who was now helping Maura take plates, cutlery and napkins into the dining room. He seemed to intuitively know what to do, while she was still sitting, taking it all in.

What kind of father would he be? Not that it mattered, because she'd never know. That realization brought an unexpected stab of regret, and she stood up to help, to get involved in a get-together with friends and families that, realistically, she might not experience again.

CHAPTER TWENTY-ONE

THE SUNDAY BRUNCH drifted into late afternoon with constant browsing at a buffet table that, as far as Nate could tell, never seemed to diminish. He couldn't recall a time back in Boston when he and friends, or colleagues, had ever indulged in a lazy day like this one. At the beginning, he couldn't resist checking the time on his phone, thinking people would soon realize most of the food and drink had been consumed and that it was time to leave. But eventually, he fell into the rhythm of it—the slow pace of chatting, munching on leftovers or simply lost in thought, staring into space. Which is what Annika had been doing for the past hour or more.

He figured she'd been enjoying herself, otherwise she'd have left. He was curious about her thoughts. What was on her mind that kept her tuning in and out of the conversations? Some new podcast idea? He liked to think she was daydreaming about him or the possibility of a future together because that was the road his own thoughts had traveled most of the afternoon.

But when she was holding Maura's baby, her face had signaled a different kind of pleasure, one that Nate knew nothing about. He was curious though and would have asked her what she was feeling then, but some instinct warned him that her answer might lead to a conversation he doubted they were ready for. Or perhaps he was way off base, and she was simply sated with good food and company.

His thoughts wandered too, and he missed the line that made everyone in the room laugh. They were all looking at him and for a second, he felt like an insecure teenager again, not in on the joke. Back then he usually never had been.

When Will repeated what Nate had called him after they'd rounded up the donkeys, Nate teased, "You've got the gift, Bower. I'm sure Maura and Theo could use some extra help around here."

There was a brief round of good-natured banter then that, for a minute, overwhelmed Nate with a sense of belonging—not only to the group around the table, but to Maple Glen itself. Because they were all part of the village, familiar enough with each other to know when to offer help, and when to back off. His gaze shifted back to Annika again. He'd noticed her laughing at the donkey whisperer line, but then she'd escaped into her own thoughts again, which puzzled him. He decided to see her alone later and find out what was troubling her.

The message for all to leave wasn't a subtle one. It came via baby Colin, whose tears couldn't be comforted and the strain in Maura's face was the signal. Theo arrived as people were getting coats and retrieving empty platters and dishes from the dining table.

"Oh no! Have I missed another party?" His disappointment was genuine, and Nate felt for him, especially when Maura cast a weary glance at her husband and rolled her eyes.

"Lots of leftovers though," Nate said. He placed the empty dishes and glasses on the tray he was holding into the kitchen sink and felt something more was needed from him. But what?

Annika came to Theo's rescue, with an offer that surprised Nate more than any of them. "I'd love to babysit one evening, or afternoon. Whichever you two prefer. If you leave a bottle or two, I think I can manage on my own… though maybe Nate could pitch in, too."

Fortunately, both Theo and Maura merely smiled without setting a date right then and there. The goodbyes were quick, hastened at the sight of weary parents and a wailing infant.

When Nate stepped outside, he paused on the sidewalk to let the chilly late autumn air breeze through and around him.

"I almost feel like a nap," murmured Annika, coming up behind him.

Nate smiled. "For a minute there, when you were cradling baby Colin, I thought both of you were about to nod off."

"So true." She buttoned up her jacket, holding the lapels tight around her neck.

"Did you drive with anyone?" he asked.

She shook her head. "I wanted to walk, but it wasn't this cold earlier."

"Why don't we walk back together, then? Unless you want to wait for Will and Leni to give you a lift. I have to pick up the cruiser at the community center."

"Sure," was all she said.

Nate decided her impassive face was a good sign and held out his arm. They strolled down the long drive leading up to the Danby farmhouse like a couple familiar with one another's gait. A couple who'd walked in such a manner many times before, Nate was thinking, although it wasn't the case at all.

After a few minutes, he said, "I think Maura and Theo will be very good parents."

The comment stopped her, and she looked up

at him, frowning. “Of course they will. What makes you say that?”

He paused, fearing he’d blundered in some way. He tried to make light of it. “No reason, only that…you know…not all parents are good parents.”

She stared up at him, waiting for more explanation. Or so he guessed. “Is it telling,” she started to say, “that of all the many conversations we’ve had since meeting, the topic of our parents has never arisen?”

“Maybe we haven’t depleted the fascinating subject of ourselves,” he joked.

At least she smiled. “True…and I guess if…you know, there was a special reason for us to talk about them, we would have.”

He couldn’t envision what that reason might be. Even something as far-fetched as an engagement wouldn’t have necessarily involved parents because of their ages. Nate saw where he was going then and decided to change the subject.

But she went on to say, “I think you know more about me and my background than I do about yours.”

“Uh, well a bit. Only what I’ve heard from Finn and Devon, along with some information from—”

“The grapevine?” she asked.

"Part of small-town life, isn't it? Only in other places, the gossip mill has other names."

"Definitely. Gossip is everywhere."

As they continued walking, Nate wanted to ask how she'd felt discovering the truth about her half-sister and even more, her father—Blake Morrison—with his long-kept secret. It seemed they'd reached a place in their relationship where those types of questions naturally occurred. But then he'd be obliged to reveal his own patchwork background. Best not go there, yet.

Time to change the subject. "Are you currently working on the same podcast series? I know you were considering the one about scammers and victims of scams that we collaborated on, and that airing it is on hold for now because of the pending fraud case."

"I sent another idea to Venture Media, the company that bought some of our *We Reveal It* episodes, but I haven't received any feedback yet."

"*Our* episodes?"

"A very good and old friend of mine—Liz Weston. She's gone on to other things at the moment, because I'd been taking a break from writing. Until that whole thing with The Seekers."

"Will you stick with podcasts, or maybe get into other types of media?"

"I'd like to keep going with the podcasts, because I spent so much time learning about them and polishing my—"

"Technique?"

She saw his grin and smiled. "There's a definite technique and approach to the narration. Along with research, of course."

"So airing them is different from—" he thought for a minute "—say, posting something quick on social media."

"Definitely, although topics vary. Some focus on true crime and others on—"

"The supernatural?" he quipped.

She got his reference. "Yeah, a case in point about legitimate podcasts, and those aimed at the sensational. Same goes for blogs, like the one The Seekers had."

"Tell me about your new idea."

"It's still in development and I haven't sent it to Venture Media yet, but the subject matter will have a broader audience and pertains to this part of the country."

"Sounds interesting. Can you tell me if I swear not to let the cat out of the bag or whatever cliché you want to use?"

That brought a laugh. "Hopefully no clichés, except for the subject of a current investigation into misuse of public funds by a local politician."

"Now you've got my interest." He held up his palm. "Scout's honor."

"Were you even a Scout?" she asked, laughing.

"Yes, but as a police officer I also know how to swear an oath and keep a promise."

"Okay, I trust you on that, Nate Gallagher."

Her smile was a mix of teasing and affection, and Nate hugged her. He could have stood there with her in his arms until nightfall if she hadn't gone on to say, "The politician's name is Paul Clarkson, and I have a feeling that media interest—not only mine—will lead to his eviction from office."

Nate closed his eyes, hoping the sickening dizziness he was feeling would subside. When he felt he could speak in a normal voice, he said, "Please don't write about Paul Clarkson."

He knew from her instant reaction—pulling away to stare up at him, incredulity all over her face—that he ought to have been more subtle.

"What? Where's that coming from, Nate?"

"I…uh… I'd rather not say right now, but maybe hold off on it for a while?"

"I'm already doing the research, Nate, and I'm positive I'll get the okay. You need to tell me what's going on."

But he couldn't. Too many memories he wanted left in the past and truths he had yet to learn. "Look, trust me on this, Annika. Hold off on it or at least let me see what you've written before using it."

"Then tell me what's going on. And why all the secrecy?"

"I can't discuss it. Not yet. I need to figure some things out."

"Like what?"

"Like how things in my life might be affected by that story." He saw she was even more bewildered. "As I said, just trust me."

"Okay…but are you trusting me, at this very moment? *Trust* is more than a word, you know, and it works both ways." She swung around and continued walking ahead of him along Church Street.

Or marching, Nate thought, watching her stiff-backed stride until she headed up the drive to her cottage and disappeared from view. He wished now he'd taken time to absorb her news and its potential consequences rather than immediately insist she hold back on writing the podcast without any explanation from him.

But all he could focus on at that moment was his mother, her name cropping up somewhere in Paul Clarkson's online bio. He hated the idea of his loving, warm mother linked to a potential felon like Clarkson, even if she'd left the marriage years ago. The possibility that his own name could eventually surface, too, was troubling. He had a year to go as interim sheriff in a place he'd grown to love, and he knew in his heart he wanted to stay. But not at the risk of his mother's past or his real father's identity whispered throughout the valley. Being the focus of gossip had been stressful enough when he'd been with Boston police, and he'd solved that problem by resigning. Despite his desire to continue as sheriff in the valley, he'd be torn if he had to choose between his dream job and keeping his mother's memory out of the gossip loop.

ANNIKA PUTTERED AROUND the cottage, straightening picture frames that weren't askew and rearranging the shelf of spices in the galley kitchen. Anything to keep busy, and her mind off the way she and Nate had parted after the brunch. What hurt most of all was his assumption that she'd betray his trust. She'd simply wanted an explanation for withholding the podcast, which wasn't unreasonable. Their disagreement over such a basic and, what seemed to her, inconsequential, matter was what really worried her.

How could they be true partners if one of them favored privacy while the other one—her, she admitted—wanted forthright and transparent communication? The disparity between their strong character traits didn't bode well for a permanent relationship. She wasn't naive enough to believe that people could easily change their inner selves, because change depended on so many factors. Foremost was the desire to change and next, the willingness to do the necessary work. At the end of the day, she was still left with the ultimate question—did she and Nate have a future together if neither was willing to change? When she heard a light tap at her front door later that afternoon, Annika knew she wouldn't have to wait for the answer.

"I need to tell you something, Annika, to explain my reaction to your new podcast idea."

His eyes reflected a misery that tugged at her heart and every nerve in her body seemed to come to a standstill.

"Do you want to come in to talk?"

He hesitated, then shook his head. "It's been a long day and we can discuss what I tell you at length tomorrow. I just didn't want to leave you imagining all kinds of reasons why I got upset when you revealed your podcast idea. The thing is…" He paused to take a deep breath, "Paul Clarkson was once married to my mother. For three years, when I was ten until I turned thirteen. They had an amicable divorce and although I never learned the details, looking back now, I suspect his willingness to bend rules when it came to business deals might have had something to do with their falling out. All that's in the past now, but, to be honest, I want the story to stay there. The idea of my mother's connection to that man becoming a source of public speculation and gossip in New Hampshire and—even worse— here in Maple Glen…"

He didn't need to say anything more, because everything in his mind and heart was etched in his face. Annika reached for his hand and drew him close, wrapped her arms around him, and never wanted to let go.

CHAPTER TWENTY-TWO

NATE REFOLDED HIS mother's letter and stowed it carefully in his shirt pocket. He felt as if he'd been swept up by a tornado, swirled high into the air and plunked down on ground that continued shaking. He had no idea what it would be like to experience an earthquake either, and prayed he'd never find out, because the tremors from the afternoon were ongoing. *Aftershock*, he thought, an appropriate term for what he was feeling. Then he told Annika everything.

When he showed her the letter, her first question was, "What's the worst that can happen?"

He liked that she was helping him review the idea without making a judgment about it or giving advice. "Walter might refuse to believe what my mother wrote and might even deny knowing her."

"Are you prepared for that possibility?" Annika asked.

He nodded because he didn't trust himself to speak. No matter how the confrontation went and what decisions followed, Nate knew he'd never forget Annika's instant embrace when he'd stood on the threshold of her cottage door, his eyes red and still damp from emotions he'd long buried.

"Do you want me to come with you?"

He hadn't, but only because this part of his search had to be private. The walk to and from Walter's alone would give him time to get his emotions in check and to plan his next steps. Whatever happened, knowing Annika would be waiting for him was the winning lottery ticket.

Church Street was deserted at dusk and Nate appreciated the solitude of the long walk to Walter Ingram's. He doubted he'd be able to handle the inevitable small talk that seemed to be a trademark of Maple Glen. Probably he'd become accustomed to those small-town pleasantries, maybe even come to appreciate them for their genuine sincerity, if a future with Annika was possible.

When he reached the end of Walter's driveway, he paused to read the sign—Walter's Honey—wood-burned by hand, Nate guessed. It reminded him of the carved birds and waterfowl he'd seen displayed throughout Walter's living area, the day he'd gone with Annika, the first face-to-face meeting with him. Amelia Owens had been there, too, and Nate recalled his speculation about the relationship between her and Walter. So many questions had since been answered, except for the two deepest in Nate's heart.

How did Walter meet Catherine, Nate's mother, and why did he leave her? The answers were all he wanted from the man, and he wouldn't leave until he had them.

He waited a minute longer to settle his breathing, and imagined Annika behind him, urging, *You can do this!* and then he walked up the driveway. A black pickup truck was parked in front of the honey house that Nate and Annika had toured the day she'd asked Walter if she could interview him for a possible podcast about local legends. Walter's only reply—"Nope"—still amused Nate, though now he worried the man's response to Nate's revelation might be just as curt and final.

He called out when he reached the open door of the large aluminum-sided shed, or honey house and waited. The echoing tap of a cane sounded from deep inside and Nate considered entering the shed, but decided outdoors was a better option. To flee the scene if necessary? He smiled at what Annika's response might be to that and missed the sudden arrival of Walter at the shed doorway.

"Sheriff Gallagher, to what do I owe the pleasure?"

A typical question from a man whose style was decidedly old-fashioned. But Nate liked that. He walked toward Walter, feeling the weight of the letter in his shirt pocket. "Good afternoon, sir," he began, immediately cursing himself for such formality. "I…uh…came to talk to you about something."

"Oh?" Walter seemed to think for a second. "Well, come into the house and I'll put the kettle on."

It was the momentary reprieve Nate had been hoping for and he nodded, then followed Walter through the side door of the house, along a dark hall and into the kitchen. He looked around the room he'd been in not long ago, taking in once more the collections of a lifetime—books, carvings, even a display of salt and pepper shakers on a high shelf that Nate hadn't noticed on his first visit.

Walter saw him checking them out and turned from filling a kettle with water to say, "My friend, Amelia, got me collecting those. Heaven knows why." He set the kettle on the stove and ignited a gas jet beneath it.

"I assume you and Amelia have been friends for many years," Nate said as he turned around to face Walter.

"Almost a lifetime," Walter said. "But I think you already know that, because I heard you were pumping her for information about me at the community center."

Nate reminded himself not to be so trusting of older women in the future. He patted his shirt pocket, as if to remind himself why he was there.

Walter's eyes tracked the movement. "Got something you want to share?" His voice was casual as he set mugs on the table, along with a jar of honey and a small pitcher of milk.

The old man was sharp, and Nate liked that. He sat down and waited while Walter made the tea. They were both taking their time, Nate thought. Not stalling, as much as waiting for the other to go first. He decided to be that one, because it would give him the lead—the person to control the narrative. Something he'd learned in law enforcement.

After Walter set mugs of tea and a plate of cookies on the table, Nate pulled the letter out of his pocket and placed it next to Walter's mug. Walter peered down at it but didn't speak.

"This letter was with my mother's will, which I received after her death almost a year ago. This—" he tapped the letter with his index finger "—is the reason why I came to Maple Glen."

Now Walter's interest picked up, but he didn't

reach for the letter. Instead, he asked, "Are you going to read it to me, or…?"

Nate pushed the letter across the table and waited. Walter finally picked it up, his hand visibly trembling. He unfolded the letter so carefully and slowly that Nate bit down on his lip, restraining the urge to snatch it away and read the contents aloud himself. But then he'd miss seeing Walter's face as he read, and that was what he needed more anything else. Words could be ambiguous and even deceiving, but a face—in Nate's opinion—usually told the truth.

"Catherine," Walter whispered as he read. Then his head shot up from the letter. "You're…"

"Your son."

Walter placed his hands on the table for support and stood up so quickly his chair teetered behind him.

Nate saw him swaying and rushed to grasp him by his elbow and upper arm to steady him. "Easy," he said. "I've got you." He clasped Walter by his other shoulder and as the two drew closer, Nate saw tears welling up in the old man's eyes.

"Son." Walter's voice cracked and he held on to Nate until the trembling that coursed through him stopped.

Nate helped him back onto his chair, and as he stared down at the gray-haired man—his father—

he waited until he could breathe normally. "Tea?" he finally asked.

"Please," was Walter's husky reply.

When Annika failed to receive an answer to her late-night text to Nate, she took matters into her own hands and headed to Walter's place first thing in the morning. She passed Nate's house, noting it was eerily still. More troubling was the sight of his police cruiser parked in his driveway where he must have left it yesterday after he'd picked it up from the community center. Either he'd walked to the police station or hadn't reported in at all. She couldn't imagine Nate Gallagher being late for work, much less missing it altogether.

The short walk was a good way to ease her nerves. She'd encouraged Nate to reveal himself to his father and her suspicion that he might have gone to see Walter was confirmed when she saw a light on in the kitchen and, through the filmy curtains at the windows, the silhouettes of two heads. Yet she hesitated at the door, unsure if this was a right or wrong time to appear. *Then why did you come at all, Annika, if you were truly worried about that?*

Because you couldn't wait a minute longer! Patience wasn't her strong point, but caring deeply for the people in her life most definitely was. She rapped on the door and, without awaiting a "Come in!" opened it.

Both men sitting at the kitchen table looked exhausted. They also looked as if they'd shed a few tears and Annika instantly regretted barging in. She'd worried on her walk from her cottage that the lives of the two men she cared for would be irrevocably changed. And when they looked her way, she saw that she'd been both right and wrong at the same time.

Nate stood up and managed a wobbly smile. He cleared his throat, and said, "Annika, I know you and…*my father*…have already met. Come and have tea with us."

IT WAS ALMOST DUSK when Nate and Annika returned to her cottage. They stood quietly for a moment as Nate grappled with the memory of the visit with Walter—the talk and the long silences in between. Nate had clasped Annika's hand in his from the moment she sat in the chair next to him at Walter's kitchen table. He'd wanted to let her know what her arrival meant to him. A moment that they'd look back to years later, understanding again and again its significance to all their lives, long after he'd heard the story Walter recounted.

"She came with a hiking group, almost thirty-one years ago," Walter had begun once they'd had their first sips of tea, "and back then, I was a search and rescue guide and volunteer—somewhat like Finn McAllister—and they hired me to walk them through part of the Long Trail. It was a wonderfully clear autumn day and we had a terrific time. Catherine—your mother—was up for every challenge and I could have taken her all the way to the White Mountains, but the others in her group wanted to get back to their hotel in Wallingford. I saw Catherine's disappointment, so offered to take her the next morning if she was available. She said she was, we had a wonderful hike and talked about everything under the sun." Walter had paused then, and Nate had seen the mix of both happy and sad memories in his face.

"When we returned to the Glen, her group had gone on to Wallingford. It was late and we were both tired. But it was a good kind of fatigue, the satisfaction of meeting a challenge. I especially liked that in her." Another pause. "I'll spare you any embarrassing details, but we managed to find a place where we could finish our conversation and…well…where we recognized the strong pull of attraction. Not just physical, but of two like minds." Walter kept his gaze on the tabletop for a long time. "I made plans overnight, but she had, too." He raised his head, meeting Nate's eyes.

"She'd gone before I awakened, leaving nothing behind but a memory that's been with me since. I tried to find her, but there weren't the same social media things back then. I had no information about her other than her name. Catherine. That was it." He rubbed his face, etched with fatigue and perhaps, the pain of remembering.

Nate thought later about choices people make when faced with decisions. He wondered what spurred some to make bad choices while others let their hearts and minds work together for the better good. His mother had decided to return home rather than stay with Walter, unaware that she was now carrying his child. She'd also chosen to keep her child and raise him alone, when she might have gone back to Walter and had a different life. Nate had made the choice to take a job in Maple Glen so that he could find, and perhaps connect to Walter, his biological father. And after their long talk, Nate knew he'd made the right decision.

Nate realized from Walter's face that the man needed some time alone. "Annika and I should leave now Walter. I think we're all exhausted." He stood up and smiled at Walter. "But I promise you I'll be back soon, to begin making up for our lost years together. I'm impressed by your wood carvings and would be interested in finding out if I've inherited that particular talent from you."

He glanced at Annika and noticed that she was tearing up again. The promise of new hope wasn't to be underestimated, Nate was thinking. Perhaps there was still a chance for them, after everything that had been said and done.

CHAPTER TWENTY-THREE

NATE WALKED HER home from Walter's, and the crisp night air seemed to recharge both of them after the honest but emotional conversation they'd had. She thought he might kiss her at the door, but he surprised her by asking, "Want to come to the Shady Nook B and B?"

There must have been enough moonlight for him to see her face, because he added, "Uh… there's something I want to show you and—" he stared up at the sky "—this is the perfect night for it."

"Okay," she said, unsure what she was getting into, but she had the feeling life with Nate Gallagher was always going to hold surprises.

He clasped her hand in his and led her back down her driveway, onto Church Street and to the B and B, almost at its end. He must have noticed the apprehension in her face because he added, "It's okay. I cleared this with Bernie the other day, when I happened to check the weather forecast and saw tonight was going to be cloudless."

Annika looked up. He was right about the clear sky, though he hadn't mentioned the moon. She pointed to it.

"Oh yes, that too, but this is different."

He didn't speak again until they arrived at the B and B front door, and he quietly turned the handle, opening the door. When he held an index finger to his mouth, her stress level hiked until she guessed he'd been doing some planning with Bernie. But for what purpose?

She followed his lead, treading as carefully as possible up the staircase to the third floor where he stopped. She came up beside him and saw a small ladder hanging down from the ceiling.

"It's okay," he whispered. "Bernie knows all about this and we both know the ladder's safe. You go first, and I'll be right behind you."

A good move, Annika thought. If she fell, she'd have something soft to land on. But she'd managed this ladder all on her own, not long ago. The night her curiosity had led her up to the roof where she'd spotted a telescope, all set up for spying. She grasped the sides of the ladder with both hands and started climbing. When her head emerged into the cupola, or whatever it was called, she saw that the door leading from it to the actual roof was open. She was tempted to turn around to ask what was going on, but she sensed that would ruin a surprise, and Nate liked surprises.

The air was brisk. November had arrived and so, too, would Thanksgiving, along with Devon's wedding. Annika hoped to come back for that, but there remained many questions yet to be answered. Like where she'd be, what would she be doing and where would she be living? The one certainty was that she would not be writing a podcast about political corruption, or even about a local legend and hero.

"What is it?" Nate hissed from below when she paused on the top rung of the ladder.

"I…uh… I don't know. I just feel—"

"Anxious about what lies ahead? Not the rooftop, but your future?"

She turned around to look at him. "Yes," she said, her voice low but clear.

"Don't be. It's all good."

His tender smile was the encouragement she needed to take the last step and walk through the door. She heard him coming up on the ladder behind her, but her thoughts were focused on the telescope at the edge of the roof. Was this some kind of joke, she wondered? A replay of that first night, when she'd interrupted his stargazing?

He reached the top and came up beside her. "Come, I want to show you something you missed the first and last time we were on this roof together." He clasped her hand and led them to the telescope, where she now saw two folding chairs. "Sit," he said, gesturing to a chair on one side while he took the other.

He spent a few minutes playing with knobs on the telescope and peering through it a couple of times until he seemed satisfied. The smile he gave her more than compensated for the chilly night air.

"Come closer—look through here," he murmured, pointing to a lens, "and tell me what you see."

She did, but couldn't speak, entranced by the swirl of starry shapes and blobs of light that pulsed in the dark heavens, or perhaps, they were simply twinkling. "It's beautiful! But what am I looking at?"

"The Fireworks Galaxy, also known as NGC 6946, but I prefer its common name, because the spiral is a childhood memory of fireworks way down here, on earth."

"Tell me more." She looked up at him from the telescope.

"I could go on all night about it, but I've something better to do right now." He stood up and fished around in his fleece jacket pocket.

Annika wasn't adept at recognizing constellations or galaxies, but her intuitive skills were excellent. She smiled at the small velvet-covered box and gasped when he opened it.

"A miniature galaxy," she whispered.

"The closest I could get."

The bright yellow diamond sparkled in the moonlight and Annika gasped when he removed the ring from its box, mostly because his hands were shaking and she feared it would fall into the oblivion of Church Street below. But he paused to take a calming breath, she guessed, and in a voice that quavered with a mix of hope and uncertainty, asked, "Will you marry me?" When she didn't answer right away, he said, "Please? So we can spend the rest of our lives together here, in Maple Glen."

She held out her left hand for him to slip the ring on. It would have to be taken in a bit, she was thinking, but right then, it was perfect. She looked up from admiring the ring to his handsome face.

"That's a deal, Sheriff Gallagher," she murmured as his lips found hers.

EPILOGUE

NATE ZIPPED UP his jacket and stared down at his police-issue winter boots. The memory of wearing sneakers mere weeks ago while searching for Stanley Wolchuk on the Appalachian Long Trail with Finn McAllister brought a smile. What a newbie he'd been then. Not that he was now an expert on Vermont weather or the state's customs and traditions, but he did consider himself "almost" a local when it came to the flora, fauna and the peculiarities of Maple Glen. Truth was, he figured that qualifying word *almost* would probably be tagged onto him for a long time.

If there was one thing he'd learned since taking up residence in Otter Valley and running the regional police station, a person didn't earn the moniker *local* until years had passed or dues were paid. He figured those dues had been paid and then some, given his accomplishments as interim sheriff since the end of October. And he was still here, the day before Thanksgiving, and still unaccustomed to Vermont winter, though he realized the light snowfall overnight was merely a harbinger of what would inevitably come.

He'd never been a fan of winter, a season that was seldom picturesque in Boston where he grew up, but he supposed by the time he was accepted as a genuine local in Maple Glen, he'd be used to all the various weather systems in Otter Valley. Still, he was looking forward to summer when the loose ends of everything that had happened in Maple Glen since Halloween would be relegated to the past, and a new future for everyone lay ahead. Without snow.

Devon and Finn were getting married on Saturday and were already living in the renovated Manor where the wedding reception would take place. Annika was still in their stone cottage, now with Marion McAllister, Finn's sister, Roxanne, and niece Kaya. Nate bet that arrangement would change quickly after the wedding due mainly to the limiting size of the cottage. Meanwhile, the rest of his belongings, including the one good suit he owned, had been shipped from Boston last week, so he was all set for the big day.

Finn had refused an offer of a stag party and Devon, likewise, a bridal shower. "Keep it simple, please," they'd both protested when Will and Leni Bower had broached the subject. Instead, the couple requested a big family dinner on Thanksgiving Day. They considered all their friends—old and new—as extended family and when Annika told him he, too, was invited, Nate had turned away, hiding the unexpected emotion in his face. The concept of an extended family was still new to him, but he embraced it without any hesitation. He had yet to accept the Glen grapevine as a fact of life in Maple Glen, though he supposed eventually he'd assume the attitude of the valley's longtime residents with a shoulder shrug and a sigh, as if to say, "what can you do?"

Because the station would be closed on the holiday tomorrow, Nate decided he'd drive a circuit around the valley after lunch, ensuring that all was well on the home front. That brought a smile as he realized he was now considering the area home. He'd told Shelley to leave work early, offering to cover any calls at the station until closing time at five o'clock. In the meantime, he intended to finish up some paperwork to ensure a relaxing holiday weekend. Well, he amended, relaxed as much as possible given the detailed list of events and instructions Devon had emailed to him and Annika.

He noticed Shelley was already on duty when he arrived at the station and he pulled up next to her car. Despite the minimal snowfall, the parking lot had been cleared overnight, and knowing winter was only beginning, he was glad he'd added a plowing service to the new budget he and Shelley had prepared for the Bennington County Council. The aroma of freshly brewed coffee and a plate of homemade muffins greeted him as he walked inside and raised his spirits a notch.

Since the owners of the cars waived vandalism charges against her son in exchange for cleaning all the targeted cars and apologizing in person to all the owners, Shelley had been showing her gratitude with frequent treats. He knew the family was continuing counseling and he bet the teen wouldn't be in trouble ever again. People were basically the same wherever they lived, Nate thought, and usually they had choices to make in their daily lives that could have an impact on family life, work or even on society in general. Hence his lack of regret for reporting the couple who called themselves The Seekers to Bennington Police.

Even Stanley Wolchuk had to account for his decision to embezzle from his own company. The man's trial had yet to begin, but Nate knew he'd be following it through media, his contacts with Bennington Police and perhaps even county scuttlebutt. Sometimes gossip was useful, if treated with the right amount of skepticism. He hadn't received notice of his inevitable testimony but figured that would happen in the coming months.

"Morning, Nate," Shelley said as he was hanging up his jacket. "Breakfast is ready."

"Aw, Shelley, you're a star!"

She shrugged, but her face shone with pleasure.

Nate knew she didn't like being the center of attention—a trait they shared—so he headed for the counter to pour the first of what he figured would be many cups of coffee throughout the day. As long as there were no emergency callouts, he reminded himself, mentally crossing his fingers as he picked up a muffin. Blueberry, he noted, and silently blessed Shelley.

"So, what's on the day's agenda?" he asked, sitting down at his desk and taking his first sip of coffee.

"Not much, Nate. I've finished typing up our new budget to Chief McNaught and printed out a copy for you to review and sign before officially emailing the digital version to him. And there are a couple of other reports to read and sign, mainly housekeeping. Receipts and such."

"Thanks, Shelley." He knew she was old-school, preferring to keep both digital and paper copies of reports, and he personally liked the custom as a safeguard against any electronic glitches. "And I'm assuming Bennington will be handling any emergency calls tomorrow and through to Monday?"

"Yes, I texted Chief McNaught's assistant and she sent confirmation that they'd be in charge from tomorrow on."

Nate felt himself relax. He'd figured there'd be no problem but wanted to make sure. He bit into the muffin as he skimmed through the receipts as well as the proposed budget. Then he logged into his computer to read his email. Chief McNaught sent a personal one, thanking Nate for his closing of the Wolchuk embezzlement case, as well as his information leading to the arrest of The Seekers. Nate was relieved to learn that the circuit judge had denied bail to all, citing the three as flight risks, but he had granted bail to Agnes Wolchuk, who'd put up the family home as collateral and turned in her passport. Nate suspected she'd been more involved than either she or Stanley had let on, but he figured the extent of her participation would be revealed at trial.

The other update he searched for in police records related to Paul Clarkson's charges. He didn't want to make direct inquiries through the county or state police networks, afraid that such interest might lead to an advantage for the defense, should Clarkson's lawyers discover Nate's former connection to the man. His worry about that possibility vanished when he saw that Clarkson had entered a guilty plea. There would be no trial, and unless some persistent journalist dug into Clarkson's history, Nate's brief connection to the man would stay in the past. Exactly where he wanted it.

Nate eased back into his chair, ate some more muffin and finished off his first cup of coffee. The day looked even more promising. He'd just finished reading his work email, most of which pertained to incidents throughout the county and not to Maple Glen, when the phone on Shelley's desk rang. She quickly looked over at him, an expression of "should I answer it?" crossing her face. Nate shrugged. They were still on duty, but he hoped the call would be inconsequential.

"Otter Valley Police, how may I help you?"

Nate watched as she listened, nodding and finally saying, "He's right here." Then she smiled and gestured to the phone on Nate's desk.

He picked up the receiver and said in his usual brisk, on duty voice, "Sheriff Gallagher speaking."

"Chief McAllister here," came a similarly brisk reply.

Nate laughed. "Hi, Finn. What can I do for you?"

"Well, you can pop by the station about four

this afternoon, if you're not involved with any policing business."

"Hopefully, I won't be. However, I am on duty until five so…"

"Call it part of your drive around before the holiday tomorrow."

"I hope this visit has nothing to do with police cruiser decorating or some such thing."

That brought a chuckle. "Nope, and there's been no Thanksgiving committee organized for us to endure, either."

Nate laughed. The village's Halloween events weeks ago had cemented the friendship between fire chief and sheriff, though afterward both men had privately vowed not to be dragged into any further schemes planned by some of Maple Glen's residents. "That's a relief. And I assume you're on duty today as well?"

"Yep, but only until end of shift about five, then Matt's taking over."

Finn's colleague and friend, Matt, had recently been promoted to captain, next in command to Finn himself.

"All right, see you about four then." After he hung up, Nate went back to the report and the budget. When he heard Shelley moving about, he glanced up to see that it was almost noon. He leaned back in his chair and stretched. "Why don't you head home now, Shelley? Things are pretty quiet and I'll make my rounds before meeting up with Finn McAllister at the fire station at four."

"Something happening there?" she asked.

Nate shrugged. "Dunno. Maybe he just wants to meet in person about any holiday plans for his department and ours. I have a feeling Bennington Police doesn't always update Wallingford Fire on schedule changes and so on."

"Hopefully that'll all change when amalgamation happens after the next election." She said, logging out of her computer. "Don't forget to take home the rest of the muffins. They won't keep until Monday, unless you freeze them."

Nate hid a smile. Mothering was Shelley's strongpoint next to administrative work, and he knew her sons were in good hands now that she'd gained full custody of them. Her ex had agreed to that condition after a counseling session, with the proviso that he would have more access in the summer.

"What're your own holiday plans?" he asked as she headed for the rear entrance to the station and her coat and boots.

"Some relaxing and finishing a book for my book club meeting next week."

"Thanksgiving dinner?"

She paused lifting her coat off the hook and turned to look at him. "You're not going to believe this, but my boys have offered to make dinner."

"Wow!"

"I think the idea came out of one of their sessions with the family counselor. They did warn me that it may not be a traditional meal, so I'm thinking something to do with pasta."

Her grin told Nate she was okay with that. "Sounds like a good step forward."

"Definitely." After she zipped up her parka, she said, "I have you to thank for that, Nate. You gave Jason a chance when you could have charged him with vandalism. George and I will be forever grateful, and the incident has made us realize we have to come to decisions and agreements that will benefit all of us."

Nate simply nodded, unable to trust himself to speak.

"I hope you have a relaxing holiday, Nate. Bye for now."

After she left, the shuffle of papers and creak of Nate's office chair echoed through the empty station as he worked steadily, reading, signing the hard copies and placing them on Shelley's desk for filing on Monday. Then he emailed the digital copies of the new report and the budget to Chief McNaught. By the time he was finished it was well past noon, and he decided to make his circuit around the station's district. Finally, there was Finn's request to see him at four at the fire station. He had no idea what that was about, but at least it was at the end of the day.

His cell phone rang as he was lifting up his jacket from a hook at the rear door and he bent down to retrieve it from the bench. He saw that it was Annika and he smiled. No doubt more items to add to his list, but he didn't mind at all.

"Hey," he murmured.

"Hey, yourself."

Her voice never ceased to warm him, and he wished he could reach through the phone to wrap his arms around her, hold on tight and never let her go. *Soon, Gallagher.*

"What's happening with you today?" he asked.

"Last-minute plans for tomorrow…and of course…the wedding."

Her voice was steady, but Nate guessed she was taking calming breaths in the pauses. "I'm booking off at four so I can help with…well… whatever." Nate grimaced at the lackluster offer, but he really had no idea what the plans were for the weekend. Her laugh was reassuring though.

"By the way, your suit arrived about an hour ago from the cleaner's in Wallingford."

"Okay, that's good so I won't have to wear my police uniform." Her peal of laughter warmed him, and he thought for the umpteenth time that they were a good match.

"Hah, that would seriously put off some wedding guests who don't know you as well as those of us in Maple Glen do."

"You mean that I'm a hard-nosed cop or a softie?"

"Officer Gallagher, Maple Glen folks know you're a softie at heart but with strong principles that aren't swayed by flattery."

Yeah, Nate thought. We really do know each other very well. "I'm guessing there may be another reason for your call. What would you like me to do?"

"Since you're closer to Wallingford than I am, could you pop into the flower shop next to the Wallingford Diner and buy some holly? Also, some boughs of pine or spruce. Devon wants to add them to the flowers for the church, to make the decorations more festive. In keeping with the season," she added.

"Uh, sure, but have those things been ordered? I mean, what if the store doesn't have any?" He was also wondering what exactly holly looked like but figured the florist would know.

"They do. Devon phoned but everyone is too busy to pick everything up and since you're the closest…plus you could get them on your way to the fire station. Right? At four o'clock?"

"How do you know about my visit to the station?"

"Um… Devon told me, when she called to ask what time I was going over to the Manor tomorrow to help with some Thanksgiving dinner prep."

"Okay," Nate said. He'd caught the hesitation in her voice and was puzzled but figured she was as overwhelmed by all the planning and instructions as he was. "So…uh…all I have to do is go to the florist and pick up the order. Right?"

"I think you can manage it, Sheriff."

She was a tease, but he liked that. Still, time was passing and he had yet to make his valley drive-around. "I'll pick up the order on my way back to the Glen. Want me to bring it to you before or after my meeting with Finn at four?"

"After."

"Right. See you later then. I'll be leaving here soon, but you can reach me by cell phone…in case there are more errands to run."

"Hah! I have to say in her defense, though, Devon is a supreme manager."

"Definitely." Nate hoped he hadn't conveyed a negative message with his quip but was reassured by Annika's next comment.

"I'll be forever grateful that you and I will view all this wedding planning with some humor…the day after the big event."

Nate smiled. Then he ventured the question

that had been on his mind off and on for several days. "What about our own plans?"

"Well...if you're referring to what I think you might be, I'm leaning toward an elopement. Maybe in the spring, followed by a nice holiday far away from Maple Glen."

They were definitely on the same page. "Sounds good to me. See you later then, and... uh...especially after all of the running around," he murmured, his tone suggesting some alone time with her ahead. A soft giggle told him she got his message.

After he hung up, he checked the time and decided to use his own car for his drive-around to save having to go all the way back to the station to exchange vehicles. As he ensured the cruiser was well locked up, he realized a garage would be an important asset and thought he'd add its construction to his budget, though no doubt he'd likely have to appeal to the Bennington County Council in person for that. All in good time, he told himself. Today was the eve of a holiday, one that involved giving thanks, and he had a lot to be thankful for.

The tour around his area didn't take long. Route 7 was almost devoid of traffic and Nate figured most people had booked off work early. If the rest of the weekend was as quiet as Otter Valley and Maple Glen were now, he was guaranteed a real holiday for himself. He made it to the florist shop in Wallingford well before three and took his time heading back to the Glen. The driveways of the valley houses were filled with cars, and lights gleamed from behind closed drapes and curtains. Daylight ended by five now, but today's already darkening sky hinted at yet another storm front moving in. Nate hoped that the weekend's celebrations wouldn't be affected by any weather system but figured nothing short of a cataclysmic event would postpone Devon and Finn's wedding.

Just before he reached the turn-off onto Church Street, he glanced to his left and saw that Walter's house was in darkness. Before moving to Wallingford with Amelia Owen, Walter had deeded the house and acreage to Nate. There were no strings attached, Walter had clarified when he and Amelia had hosted them for dinner, but he hoped that Annika and Nate—"my son" he'd murmured—might even take over the honey and beekeeping business one day. In the meantime, Walter intended to scale down the number of working bee hives on the property and make the short trip from Wallingford in the spring and summer months to manage them. Then he'd embraced Nate, holding on as if he were moving to another country instead of another town. The *son* reference had made it impossible for Nate to speak for a long moment. He was still adjusting to this new father-son relationship that and although he hadn't yet used the "father" word yet, he knew the day wasn't far away.

The plan was that he and Annika would move into Walter's house in the week or so after Devon and Finn's wedding, because the first step in Leni Bower's extension of her farm shop and its parking lot was going to be demolishing the house Nate had been renting since his arrival in the Glen. Walter had reassured Nate and Annika that they were free to tear down his house as well and build a new one of their own.

All in good time, Nate figured. He and Annika hadn't yet reached an agreeable halfway point when it came to houses and decor. She leaned more to a modern style, while he had a sentimental attachment to the past. "Old things" as she loved to tease.

Meanwhile, he had some packing to do before next week, some clothes and a few personal possessions, because the rest of his belongings hadn't arrived from his storage facility in Boston.

When he reached the fire station, he was surprised to see a number of cars parked outside. The garage door fronting the area where the pumper and secondary engine were stored was down, so Nate walked to the regular entrance of the station. He heard the rumble of voices as soon as he pulled on the heavy door, though when it clanged shut behind him all was quiet. Much later, he'd wonder if he was as good at detecting as he'd always thought, because the second he pushed open an inner door leading into the heart of the firehall, lights flashed on.

He saw the banner first, strung from one side of the room to another. *Welcome to Otter Valley and Maple Glen* and beneath those words, *Sheriff Gallagher*. Then a large easel, standing off to the right side of the banner, supported an enormous pad of paper, headed with a single word—*PETITION*. Beneath that title were dozens of signatures, though Nate didn't actually study them until much later. He stood frozen on the spot, his brain sluggishly trying to process what was happening. Nate saw Annika start toward him, but it was Finn who stepped ahead, his right hand extended.

"Welcome, Nate. You'll notice that our sign doesn't read interim Sheriff Gallagher, and that's because all of us here today—and many more residents throughout the valley—have asked Bennington County Council to forego waiting until next year's election and to officially make you our sheriff right now. We submitted a digital copy of the petition two days ago and got our reply this morning. The full-time, permanent job is yours as of Monday. Until then, you've got a long weekend to relax, get to know more Valley people and prepare for your new career."

Nate didn't need to say a word. He managed a wobbly smile and shook Finn's hand. Then everyone rushed toward him, but it was Annika who reached him first.

ANNIKA STUDIED THE extralong polished oak table in Leni and Will's new dining room. Resplendent was the best word she could summon to describe it, as well as the entire room. This was her first tour of their new home, and she loved the way the couple had integrated both their styles. Classic design in the formal living room with its adjacent dining area, and ultramodern in the kitchen and family room annex.

She moved around the table, counting the settings. Fourteen, in all. There were no printed place cards indicating where guests should sit, and Annika was happy about that. The scene looked formal, but she guessed neither Leni nor Will wanted it to be completely that way. She admired the table decorations—colorful paper autumn leaves and pumpkins handmade by Leni's children—and especially loved that Leni had adorned the table with them rather than leaving them on the younger group's table set up in front of the television in the family room.

As she walked, she mentally tallied the guest

list. Maura and Theo were coming with two-month-old Colin, who would probably be in some baby contraption, Devon and Finn, along with his mother, Marion, his sister, Roxanne, and her daughter, Kaya. Walter and Amelia had been invited, and Nate had insisted they stay overnight in Walter's former house—now Nate's—but Amelia opted for the Shady Nook B and B. A wise decision, Annika had thought, because the house was in transition and cardboard boxes, a couple of crates and many suitcases belonging to both Nate and Walter littered most of the rooms.

Leni was roasting two turkeys from her farm shop and had put together a charcuterie board appetizer for the adults, plus popcorn and potato chips for the kids. The other guests were providing various side dishes and desserts. After browsing the internet, Annika had decided to make a casserole, ignoring Nate's raised eyebrows as she began the prep work for it in the stone cottage that morning. She figured he was recalling his invite to dinner weeks ago, after they'd bumped into each other at the grocery store in Wallingford. *The frozen lasagna.* The memory prompted a smile, but she was determined to ramp up her culinary skills, especially since they'd soon be living together.

He'd offered to help chop vegetables, but she'd suggested he find Finn and Will, who'd been talking about a walk onto the Long Trail. They'd promised to keep cell phones handy and would traverse only to the first blaze mark or so, but Annika suspected they actually wouldn't get much farther than Leni's former home, where Nate had been staying until yesterday, and the large television Nate had rented for the Thanksgiving football games. Her finished vegetable casserole was now sitting on Leni's new kitchen counter, waiting to be reheated in the microwave since the two ovens were filled with the rest of the feast.

The doorbell's peal made both Leni and Annika jump. Leni looked across the kitchen at Annika, who was scooping homemade cranberry sauce into bowls. "Here we go!" she exclaimed.

"Showtime," Annika replied. She matched Leni's smile—a combination of trepidation and excitement—placed the cranberry serving spoons into the bowls and followed her to the front door.

DEVON WAS BEAUTIFUL. Make that stunning, gorgeous and all the other synonyms that applied, Annika was thinking, as she adjusted her sister's small tiara with its wisp of veil. They were standing in a corner of the church entry hall, waiting while Roxanne tucked an unruly strand of Kaya's hair behind her velvet-covered headband.

Devon had opted for a small wedding party, wanting both sides of her new extended family to be represented—Annika, the maid of honor, and Kaya, who would lead the procession as flower girl.

"You all look beautiful," Roxanne whispered before kissing her daughter's cheek and leaving to take her seat inside.

When the first chords from the organ reverberated throughout the church, Annika turned to give her sister a thumbs-up and saw Devon take a long, deep breath. "Are you ready for this, sis?"

"I am. I feel like I've been waiting for this moment all my life. Finding love and getting to keep it, forever. That's what this is all about, isn't it?" Devon gestured to their small group and the aisle leading to the altar.

As always, Devon articulated perfectly the meaning of the ceremony about to begin, and Annika thought back to the afternoon weeks ago, when she and her sister finally opened up about their pasts, their different childhoods and the quirks of fate and luck that had led them to each other. Of course, decisions and choices had been also involved in their discovery of one another.

Just then the large wooden church door opened behind them and the couple she and Devon had been awaiting stepped inside. Amelia Owen's quick smile seemed to apologize for their late arrival as she blew a kiss to Devon and hurried to take a seat inside. Then Walter appeared, cane in hand, and wearing a dark suit, white shirt and tie. He smiled at their expressions.

"Were you expecting jeans and flannel shirt?"

"Um, maybe a bee suit?" Annika quipped.

"I left it at home for you, though you may have to take a tuck in here and there."

Annika smiled at the reminder that she'd offered to manage his beekeeping business, with his guidance, in the spring, although she hoped she and Nate would be partnering with that new endeavor. She'd also be working on her new contracted podcast series for Venture Media about life in small-town America.

Walter extended an arm for Devon, who gazed up at him with all the love of a daughter. They had a connection that Annika envied, and she guessed that any future son for her sister and Finn would certainly be named after the man—a modest and humble legend in Otter Valley.

"You're going first, honey," Devon whispered to Kaya. "And don't forget to smile."

"I know," Kaya whispered back. "We had a rehearsal for this last night."

Annika grinned. Devon's eight-year-old niece—going on eighteen as Roxanne joked—was going to be a capable babysitter when Leni and Will

Bower's baby was due in the spring. Maple Glen was growing, and Annika wondered how she and Nate would fit into the village, and what their days ahead would look like.

The first chords of the traditional bridal march pealed throughout the church and shifted Annika back to the present. Heads turned toward the wedding party, and Devon nudged Kaya, who began her walk down the aisle. Finn, standing next to his best man, Will, beamed encouragement at his niece. Annika thought she saw him add a wink to the grin he aimed at her as she followed Kaya.

Muted gasps and murmurs filled the nave when Devon and Walter appeared, but it was Nate, a few rows from the front on the groom's side, whose smile struck Annika's heart as she was passing him. He pointed to his slightly raised left hand and mouthed a single word—*soon.*

* * * * *